Coyote Reloaded

OR

Mything in Action

The Metalithic Myth Motorvates!

—Nuclear Polythermic Edition—

by Yulalona Lopez

illustrated by William Washburn

Calamitosus est animus futuri anxius
Seneca

Dedications
To the *Coyote Being* behind every living being.
To *Precious Woulfe*, for being.
To *Devorah Levi*, for being enthusiastic about reading and criticizing wicked stories.

Coyote Reloaded

OR

Mything in Action

The Metalithic Myth Motorvates!

—Nuclear Polythermic edition—

Coyote tires of trying to educate people,
he tires of fighting the unmasked
monsters of modern mythology,
and he tries to retire in a tropical paradise
bounded by assholes and asphalt

Alternate Title:
Coyote Recrudescent
The Deathless Disease is Active Again

Alternate Title *Deux*:
Coyote Recherché
The Dog is Too Refined for Civilization

Written by Yulalona Lopez
Illustrated by William Washburn

Calliope Press
Mozart & Reason Wolf, Ltd
Sarasota
2010

Acknowledgments
Several of these works have been published on internet sites out of desperation for attention. So what? They were not as polished anyway.

Book Design by Ryan Garcia Calusa
Tallevast Florida
Designers@RianGarciaCalusa.com

Original drawings and illustrations copyright © 2010 by William Washburn

3 Muses Books / Calliope Press
Sarasota, Florida
Editor@3Muses.us

Mozart & Reason Wolfe, ltd.
Wilmington, Delaware
Mozart@ReasonWolf.com

Publishers Cataloging-in-Publication data Yulalona Lopez,
1969-
YulalonaLopez@Itsayaya.com
Coyote Reloaded/Yulalona Lopez
I. Title. PS3553.A644A898 2010

ISBN 0-911385-51-7 (paper)
     978-0-911385-51-9 (paper)

Manufactured in the United States of America

Correction (of the review of *Coyote Rebooted*): I meant to say 'plagiarism' plus 'original' equals 'plaginal' —I mean 'orgasm.' That makes more sense, doesn't it, I mean, really?
Claude-Marc M-P.

Contents

Preamble: Subversive Fairy Tales

The Discussants:
Captain Von Hufferin, expert on fairy tales for Huffin Mitten Co.
Joe Clerk, the 3Muses company editor
Ruwanda Washington, children's book critic for a Sarasota paper

Washington: Looky here, dese stories be way too difficult for childs. Dey
    don't want no death and cussin. Childs wants to reads bout cuddly
    rabbits or little sorcerer kids flying away on brooms from big mean
    bastard adults. I mean Coyote be using generic engineering to beat
    some ho—

Hufferin: Hey, that's my water! Give it back. Nonsense! This is how the
    young learn about death and profanity! Do you want them to learn
    from uncle Jack? These stories refract the real world, like Alice in
    Wonderland— sharpen our perception by distorting it, then teach us to
    fear it. Nothing looks the same again, and the world is slightly strange.
    I'll tell you what. Hey, my pen!—

Washington: You bald white snippet, don tell me these are incoherent and
    reversive, and I'll tell what really drills my sock—

Hufferin: Subversive?! Well, maybe they are subversive, a little. After all
    ecology is subversive, art is sub—

Washington: No, communism is submersive, the feminist movement is
    sneaky, but this is affrontive—

Clerk: Pardon me, I've turned off the recorder. I think we need to follow a few
    rules of order to present our ideas simply and coherently, so please let
    me introduce the book, and we can continue our exegesis of coyote.

       Since stories are often the most influential event in many children's
early lives, it is important to understand what stories do. Do they just
entertain? Is their purpose to provide cultural lessons or just to enchant
the developing imagination with descriptions of strange and wonderful
or dangerous and terrifying beings, from the past or from the adult
imagination?

       Coyote is subversive to the extent that his role is to show what
happens when you step outside of the rules, when you do not learn the
valuable lessons of a culture. Otherwise it would just be another boring
education pandrum with talking heads and rule-giving sermons. The
stories have to capture the imagination, so the stories are personal and
involving instead of—

Hufferin: I have my doubts about this approach—it is stale and unpopular—
    but the author does try to make them relevant.

Washington: Revelant? Huh? What good does it do to tell children how much
    fun it is to break the rules? Huh? Think about it. Society is more violent
    now because of these stories!

Hufferin: Oh, I doubt that. You must be confusing books with television. Society is getting less violent. In most countries guns are forbidden and crimes have been reduced.

Washington: Why we hear bout so much violence, then, huh?

Hufferin: Media. The irresponsible sensationalism of a free press ruled by advertising wanks to increase sales.

Clerk: Pardon me, the stories in the book?

Hufferin: The book is clever enough. The author has had fun putting Coyote into automobiles and seeing what would happen.

Washington: Too much fantasy. How can Coyote be brought back to life so easily? That is old fashioned and too silly.

Hufferin: Hey! What happened to your accent? Tell me you don't watch movies about immortal villains hacking up hundreds of teenagers at abandoned camps in an infinite series of films? Where do you think that came from?

Washington: Accent was a role I didn't like. It's fun being black. But, I think Curtis and some of the actors in those movies have established themselves well across other genres. These movies themselves—

Clerk: Speaking about Coyote, what kind of movies would these stories make?

Hufferin: I think they would be therapeutic and enlightening, because these kinds of tales are really ageless, which is why many native cultures still tell the original stories—

Washington: Actors that play burnface, leatherface and hockeymask—

Clerk: The masking theme, yes, exactly—masks are *important*—the theme has been continued for generations in stories, regardless of changes in the media and styles—

Hufferin: That is why I think these stories could be important; regardless of changes in mores and technology, the same human situations and problems still exist. Oh, my gosh, what am I saying? I'm being subverted.

Washington: These actors creating series of immortal characters who also impart lessons on—

Hufferin: On what, how dangerous it is to be young or to have fun at parties?

Washington: Don't interrupt me with your pedantic existential *crap*.

Hufferin: What does fantasy do? Fairy Tales? They filter the real world so we can make decisions easier, better decisions. That is what these stories *could* teach, if they just—

Clerk: Obviously these stories can inspire, or at least irritate, readers or listeners to have conversations about them. Perhaps they can educate the readers or listeners to—oh, wow, look at that, would you? Just a little space left. We're done.

Part 1. Ambles

Making Space for Time OR *Wakanda Mandala*

Graduation time again for the animals on the Powhattan Public Playing Field. Another year. 2010. A new class. Crow was Valedictorian, Beaver was Salutatorian.

Standing by the North soccer goal, Nature addressed the animals, "This year I'm giving out Certificates of Adaptation to those species who have survived another year of human dominance, interference and collapse. Wolf, Polar bear, Beaver …" and she listed them all.

"What about me?" asked Coyote interrupted.

"Well, I do have recognition for coyote, termite, rat, ant, opossum, kudzu— but, you guys are thriving for the moment, so no big deal."

"No big deal? I survive because I'm clever, not because Spirit gave me long legs, camo fur—

"Big nose?" Nature asked.

"Big nose, hey!"

"Giant radar-dish ears?"

"Okay, so where's my certificate?" Coyote asked

"Okay, here, don't chew on it," and she started calling the animal names by size, just to thin the crowd before she got to Bacteria and Viruses, "Bluewhale, Spermwhale …"

"Um, hello," started Elephant, "the whales could not get here. Seaturtle, over there, has agreed to deliver their uhh paper. Waterproof?"

Nature nodded and restarted with Elephant.

Coyote sat down next to his mate and unrolled the diploma. It said, 'Golden Toad,' and Coyote started to protest, but Wakanda put a donut in his open mouth, and whispered, "Goldy didn't make it." Wakanda clapped with the others, thinking about the animals that were missing, River Dolphin, Black Rhinoceros, Javan Tiger, Pyrenean Ibex, and the bees, bats, frogs, and others unable to compete in a fully processed, poisoned, industrial, digital world.

"I don't see Spider. Where is spider?" Badger asked.

"That dammed invertegrate never repays my favors. He really gets on my nerves," Coyote said, spraying donut crumbs on his friends.

"Maybe you ate him?" Otter suggested.

Badger narrowed his eyes and asked Coyote: "How come you wear so many masks? You're always getting eaten when you do."

"That's stupid. Most of the time I'm the eater, but, yet," and Coyote paused philosophically in his Bertrand Russell mask, "nature is one big game of rock, paper, scissors. It's a circle. Everyone gets eaten eventually. It's fun!"

          "What's scissors?" Badger asked.

                    "You're crazy!" Otter said.

   "—fun, like going down a tube of water. Oh, it hurts sometimes, but then you come back. Masks let you come back, let you be everything in turn, let you be wise—oh, heck, ask any human kid."

                 Badger nodded at Coyote's wisdom. Otter groaned at Coyote's bullshit and made choking noises.

     Crow came over, and Coyote greeted him, "Oh, brilliant Crow, finder of the food of others, how can we praise you enough?"

                  Crow accepted this adulation as the others patted him on the back, not noticing the new paper sign stuck there that said, "Eat me!"

Wakanda let Coyote go off with Badger and Otter for a few drinks. She felt alone for a moment, but wondered how things had changed so quickly in the past 100 years. Then, she wondered where she could go, now.

     She calculated 135,000 years ago, the time of her ancestor coyotes. The grasses had been pushed south by the ice, the forests pushed further by the cold and dryness. Then, she was there. The winds from the north were cool and the sun seemed smaller, although she knew it should be the same. She went out on a broad field sloping down to a river. She figured it must be Manitoba since she had shifted north as she went back through ordered time. She lay in the sun until she could see a mouse shuffle ten lengths away. She raced to the mouse and got it, then hunted down 14 others. Then she slept in the sun, until it was dark. Wakanda thought the days were shorter in this past. Where were the other Coyotes? Were they further south?

     How could she travel in time and space? How could she do it? Could others do it? Could she find them? Her thoughts returned to the actual shifting: How could she do it? At first she had thought of time and space as a giant house; she was simply visiting other rooms when she moved; some of the rooms were in the past or far away. She still did not understand how she moved. As she learned more about the universe, she realized that the house was falling apart at one end and being added to on the other.

     She visualized a different approach. Maybe shifting was more like weaving a carpet with a knotted weave. The carpet is being woven by all the living beings and chemical processes, making knots by living, wrapping the strands from warp yarns, weaving in groups, compressing. Maybe the physicists were right and the world was made of strings! The carpet was so long that the older parts fell apart and blew away. When she moved across the pattern, what she was doing was mentally putting together the threads that had fallen apart. She was able to trace them and hold the old patterns somehow. Perhaps that was the reason her worlds were so simple—she had been unable to tie all the threads together—just some of them, enough for a simple world.

Because she did it that way, she realized that she could never affect the future, which was always being made of the present, never the past, no matter how many mice she ate or what she did or mixed up. There was no paradox, just independent shifts.

She looked up again at the clouds forming and changing and dissipating. It was so wonderful to see the patterns. As she looked, the patterns became more complex, almost mathematical. She saw one. It looked like an image like a mandala, but she could expand it to many dimensions by following the lines and curves. Was she tracing the pattern of the universe? The hidden geometry of space-time? Was that what resonated with her brain, her neural networks? So, the grass she was sitting on was a thoughtform? But, it was real; she was real as far as she could tell.

She decided to see if she could find other patterns like that. She closed her eyes and came back to the graduation field. She looked at the patterns around the others, then around Coyote. … Ah, here was a promising thread. It led her to a strange digital world, inside a computer, where she saw Coyote again. Coyote in a computer? What was she seeing? Coyote was implementing a complex algorithm. He then input the data for a large connected complex that seemed to have real multidimensional forms. She decided to look closer.
"Hey, which avatar are you?" D-Coyote asked?

"Mrs. Finch," Wakanda answered, "I'm one of the programmers."
"Hey, you're hot. Wanna see my Marscapes?"

Obviously, this avatar was closely related to Coyote. Wakanda asked, "You were programmed, too? Who did you?"

"Don't know. I just see the initials on the code notes, SPRT. Mars is great, though, you have to see this!"

"Sure, I haven't seen it from this angle," Wakanda answered.

"Let's start over here with the mission objectives. This is of course only one scenario. I think, no wait, let me reboot, first." And D-Coyote twisted his lip around his teeth.

Wakanda thought he had the same mannerisms as her mate. She intended to ask him how he got here and what he was doing. But, might as well see the show first.

"See from the Orbiter here, we will take a shuttle down to Mare Voluminaris, and disembark …"

Wakanda was amazed by the clarity of the view of the Martian surface—she could almost see winds stirring some of the patterns of dust—and by the sophistication of the program. She wondered if this program be enhanced could extrapolate into the past or future, or did that require the wilder imagination of a master weaver.

Visit from Hank-Ra OR *Global Warning*

Coyote strolled into Powhattan, not bothering with a mask or disguise. His stomach was still gurgling from the graduation celebration. Too much beer. He had been drinking happily until Fox told him about his new theory of human civilization—it was just to create beer, to domesticate conscious-altering suds with a still in every house, for convenience, daily inebriation, and a few extra vitamins by accident. Then Fox claimed—Coyote couldn't remember, but it had put him to sleep until now.

He saw a strange group by the 'Stop-on-Inn' and decided to check them out. "Hey, it's Hank-Williams. Hey, how's the fifth wave of gods developing?" Coyote asked.

Hank-Ra's eyes narrowed at the insensitive string of errors and insults, and he reached for his gun, but his hand got caught on his flowery Ralph Lauren cowboy shirt. He flushed and put his hand behind his back, then he answered. "Seems to be slow coalescing, but we're working on it, you incoherent clod."

Coyote nodded, sorry that these new waves were trying to replace him, "I'm into incoherence. Coherence is overrated. Incoherence is creative, stimulating—"

"Cheap dipstick," muttered Hank-Ra.

Coyote was quiet, wondering if 'dipstick' was an insult. He was a first wave animal god, still potent, still persuasive, and still around. "Who's that with you? Your hit team?"

"Yea, these are my guys. Fellow Egyptians who serve me. This is Osorkon and Tawosret."

Coyote recognized the species—bull-necked enforcers. Then he asked about the third man, "Who's that?"

"That's Metjetji, the aesthete."

"Oh, what sport is his specialty? Fencing?"

"Sport? No, no. He senses things, feels things."

Metjetji spoke, "We're here to warn you to stay away from the chambers of the gods."

"If you mean the Masonic Lodge in Atchison, the food's not that good anyway. Humanity goes for cheap quantity, like an elephant or whale."

"*No!* You will not diss Humanity. She is a great god, in a class by herself!" protested the red-faced aesthete.

"That's because she ate the rest of the class. Look, don't give me warnings. I have my own team of hitters. Heavy ones. Unlikeable ones. You don't want to meet them in the dark."

"Who? Bat, snake? Fox, maybe Chigger?" Hank-Ra snickered.

"Did Humanity put you up to this? Is she still fat? Who elected her Queen? I have a right to a podium, just like any legitimate god. In fact, I am one of the oldest and most respected."

"Yea, right; none of the others have a cartoon named after them. Oh, I'm sorry, you're just a bit player in the Roadrunner cartoon. You're just an extra in my scene, too. Everyone is just an extra somewhere. Heh, heh. Listen! I'm not joking around. We are trimming the ranks of nonproductive gods. You're gone. That idiot Nature is gone, and Weather, too—too flighty her. We are taking in the old durable gods, like Thor and Uzume. We are sponsoring new gods, like Engineer and Web. This will be a collusion of strengths. We will rule every living Being on the planet. Everyone will have his or her own god to worship. You have been warned!"

Coyote looked at the slit-eyed cat, with an arched back and unsheathed claws. Suddenly, Coyote threw a ping-pong ball against the restaurant wall and watched for a second as Hank-Ra automatically raced to it and batted it to one of his henchanimals. Coyote took that opportunity to vanish into the fields.

What he found was another Egyptian god lying in the wheat field.

"Hi, I'm sunlight personified," Re said.
"We are all sunlight changed and captured in cycles," Coyote noted, "well, a temporary stop to coolness anyway, before we let it go and someone else captures part of it." What was this? Egyptian Day in Wheatland, Kansas?

"Hey, really, I'm sunlight, really," Re announced.

Coyote thought: The gods all fail one by one, but we invent new ones with the same clay feet. Must be a limit of our imagination. But, how did some old gods get back? Must be reused old clay. So, Coyote watched Re basking in the sun, "Hey, you know Hank-Ra?"

"Some upstart hybrid twit. No style."
Coyote lay down next to Re grateful for a sympathetic ear. "You know what that little pipsqueak was trying—"

Hank-Ra:
Part cowboy
Part catgod
All plotter

Toth the Egyptian Tipster

"I saw the god Coyote. He was horrible. Old, torn, dirty, drooling, fluids everywhere. All the power hid behind a word or symbol, forced out with the drool and spittle. He looked foolish and quaint, but when he gestured some terror rose out of the sun, in daylight, manifested itself in a dark and ragged form. I ran. I was not ashamed. What I saw was beyond some secret darkness."

"It's okay Mr. Mouse. You're back in the hole, safe and noisy."
Suddenly a giant paw swept the mouse into a drooling maw.
'Oh, shit!' thought Misses Mouse as she leaped down the tunnel.

Coyote was up before dawn, thinking—that was new—about what was happening to Kansas, the fields, the pollution. What kind of place was it for pups? Were there enough mice for everyone? He spit out a stringy tail. He decided to go over the hill and watch the sunrise. He left the den and went up the slight rise. He saw Wakanda sitting on the crest of the hill, Slightly below her was a monkey—Sun Wukong? No wrong shape, wrong smell. From the back it looked kind of like a small lion, then it turned and looked at him, the long face framed with wild grayish hair, showing long teeth.
As it spoke to him, "صباح الخير."
Wakanda spoke, "Itsayaya, this is Djehuty, who has come from Egypt to study here."

Then, Djehuty turned and started howling, "Owwwwwww, Owwwuh," as the sun started rising.
Wakanda started howling, "Yip Yi yi yi."
Coyote rolled his eyes, "Hey Duhuti sans blowfish, what are you studying?"
They ignored him and kept howling until the sun was all the way exposed by the turning of the earth. The baboon and Wakanda sat facing Coyote.

Wakanda said, "Djehuty is known as 'Toth' in Greek and English. He was vizier to Re the sun god, the record-keeper for the other gods, and a god himself, of the moon and magic, writing and wisdom.
Coyote could not quite meet the other's eyes. "Well, that explains the bronze surfer guy yesterday sneezing and rolling over. Why are you here?"
"To learn stories, the many stories of this continent."
"Hmmm," said Coyote. "Are you, like, the Monkey Prince? You should start with the stories of Coyote, Raven, and Turtle."

Later, Coyote said to his mate. "Why should I be nice to some foreigner named Sloth?"
"Toth. Because he is a trickster and he has bigger teeth than you. He can be terrible if he chooses."

"Oh, what are his tricks? Wagging that humongous rump?"

"He can become the shape of a bird or a man. He is good at talking, playing games, and measuring."

Playing games? Maybe Coyote could get Tothy interested in playing a few of the web games on the computer. But, what could he win from Coyote? A life? A mask? And, what could Coyote win? Access to Egyptian secrets? The ability to howl at light?

The next morning, in the same field, when Coyote saw Toth, he asked, "Hey, ever played computer poker?"

"Listen, C-boy, I like you, so I won't try to kill you. We have some things in common, so I wanted to warn you to beware of Seth."

"I'm not afraid of any god named Beth."

"Seth, it's 'Seth' and he's a heartless killer," Toth said.

"Okay, so he's an Aardvark biller or something. I'll punch him in the snout and kick him back to his burrow," Coyote boasted, "And that's the way it will happen!"

"Don't trust him or underestimate him," Toth warned. "You're just an obstacle or quick buck to him."

Coyote shrugged and sat down and looked at the baboon.

Seth asked, "You know where computers are?"

And, Coyote loped off, followed easily by a large, white bird, who was saying, "I have to check my email. The UN barrister says that I may have inherited a million dollars from an African Prince."

Seth the Face of Death

Coyote watched as the strange dog trotted towards him. It was coming in a straight line but its legs seemed to cross sometimes, giving it an odd gate. It had an odd color, red, like an Irish dog. As it got closed Coyote noticed that it had a long, curved, pointed snout and tall Coyote-like ears, but strangely squared. There was something odd about the tail; it seemed tufted but also forked. Jackal maybe.

"Now what?" Coyote thought. Another trickster come to sit at the feet of the master, him, of course? Coyote gave a formal bow on his front legs.

A strange wind blew up a small cloud like fog, making the day seem darker. The other bowed slightly, then stood still. Coyote wanted him to come closer to pay homage to Coyote, but the other stood there, ignorant of protocol. Coyote approached and the other held his neck to one side, which Coyote interpreted to mean subservience.

When Coyote approached, the other suddenly grabbed Coyote's throat and suffocated him. *Ohumphh uhohhohh*—Coyote twisted and turned desperately rolling to try to break the hold, but it was no good, he could not breathe. He could only watch as the other tore him apart, tearing off the legs and then the head, then hacking the body into pieces, before finally speaking to the dismembered Coyote parts, "I am the stronger god, the master of the eternal forces of chaos and destruction. Hank-Ra's sister, Mer-seti, said you would be a worthy foe, A trickster like me, master of the desert, god of disorder and war. Not so. I am not here to learn, just to turn your rich black soil into my poor red desert soil. I know you can see me and hear me for a while. I will not scatter your parts to the corners of the world. I have learned a new strategy—acid. Yes, just acid. There will be no Horus or Fox to bring you back to life. Even your molecules will be broken into elements. Your spit will just be water, your hairs just broken bits of protein. Ha! I may drink—"

Coyote's last thought before darkness, was 'what a frigging blowhard. That wasn't fair, pretending to be submissive. Later, he would crush—'

Seth gathered up all the pieces and wrapped them in plastic, which he took to a train yard near Kansas City and looked for a rail car filled with acid. He went towards the end. He couldn't get the first lid off so he went to the last car. *Mreechuhtink!* He got it off, dumped the bag of body parts in, and slammed the lid—*Kreeeklang!* That was easy: "Good-bye Coyote."

He went to look for Wakanda, whom he had heard was a more accomplished work of art altogether for an opponent, maybe even worthy of killing.

The train pulled out slowly, with its seven cars, on the way to Kansas City to pick up more and take them to Chicago. The first six cars were filled with hydrochloric acid, but, unbeknownst to Seth, who could not read English or Spanish, the seventh was Kapton, a polyimide made by Dupont Hitachi for use in flexible printed circuits for computers.

Later in the dark of the womb-like tank, a dream came to Coyote's spirit. He was whole again, but not exactly alive. He seemed to be an orange snake in dark water. And, he was growing longer as the water invaded him. How long would he grow? What would happen to him? Would he be able to get out? What would Fox do, eat the snake or jump over it? Then he became quiet again and spread out into the strange fluid of life.

Wakanda
jumps time
to escape
Seth

Reamble: Seth & Wakanda

Wakanda saw the unfamiliar figure trot towards her. She recognized something odd about it and shifted out of the way—far out and far away. Aardvark/dog was what she thought. She remembered Hank-Ra's predictions of the confluence of gods and realized that she needed to prepare thoroughly to protect her family.

She shifted. It was a strange experience, so she tried to understand it. It was all colored threads, moving, separating recombining, Being pulled from the future and pushed into the past, gossamer hair thin or worm-fat, a fractal labyrinth of capillaries, knots forming and dissolving as everything was pulled into the present, patterns being formed in multiple dimensions, some attractors, some repellers, it was information and deformation and reformation, and she could touch all of it, almost direct it like some mad spider. There were seven more dimensions, but she had trouble differentiating between them—once she saw her self, or her mind's image of her, all sides even the insides visible at once, trying to trace a mass of threads into the past. In the distance at both ends it looked like luminous smoke.

She travelled back in time and space to spend a few weeks in Nubt, in pre-Dynastic Egypt, 5100 years ago. The red lands were divided by a black strip along the river. The flooding Nile renewed the black land. Through time, she observed Seth fall from the Osirian pantheon, slay Osiris, then be castrated and exiled by Horus. The punished sky god Seth soon became just the downward motion of the sun, the source of destructive summer heat, and always the creator of disorder.

She studied the aardvark and noticed the connections:
Aardvark was Nocturnal and lived in a burrow,
Seth travelled every night through the underworld in the solar boat.
Aardvark was associated with night, underworld and death,
And had an important symbolic role in Egyptian beliefs.
Seth was the murderer of Osiris, enemy of Horus,
and had an important symbolic role for Egyptians.
What was Seth's weakness? She had to look deeper.

Where was Coyote, or for that matter, Fox? What could she do? There was no hurry, if you could control Time, so she went back into the Kansas of 135,000 years ago, the time of Coyotes, before wolves had repopulated North America. She played and slept, and ate well. The mice were fatter and less wary. The grasses were softer; the sun was smoother.

Wakanda woke up in her den. No Coyote. She could not feel his spirit, so he must be dead again. Then she remembered the hairs in her medicine kit. At the rate he was dying, she was going to have to take another bite out his rear end to replenish her collection. Fox came by, as if by magic. She pulled out two hairs and Fox jumped over them. Wakanda wrote him a check for $100 and thanked him.

"It's for a good cause," Fox explained, "animal rights." And he jumped over the hairs.

Shwoof! Kaawauuuh! Coyote sputtered in bloom, filling out into his handsome fullness, "Agggh, what a dream! Owwow, that hurt. Who was that red bastard? Hey, what time is it? I might be late for my swearing in ceremony. Let's go!"

Wakanda and Fox knew he was looking forward to claiming his seat in Congress. Flawed elections seemed not to be a cause for concern anymore.

As Coyote raced down the hill to town, Wakanda sighed and composed her Meryl Streep mask, then started the Hummer.

Coyote had heard the engine and waited at the bottom of the hill, impatient to be picked up, "Com' on C'mon."

She stopped and jumped out of the driver's seat.

As Coyote tried to get in to drive, she tripped him and jumped on him, holding him down.

"Don't, the wheat tickles," Coyote said squirming.

"Stay still and form a mask. You can do it. I've seen you practicing."

"It's too hard, I can just use the Vincent Price rubber Halloween mask, please, there's no time."

"That's my point, no time; there's no time like the present. Now just imagine a face,"

"Who?" Coyote whined.

"See my face? Recognize it?" she asked as she rearranged her aspect.

Coyote shook his head.

"The movie?"

"Uh, *Transformers*?"

"No, *Sophie's Choice*," Wakanda answered.

"Oh, that old tearjerker."

"Remember the other actor? Imagine his face. Now imagine your muscles rearranging, imagine smooth skin, a flatter snout, shrink your facial hairs, pull your ears down. Imagine you are that person in the movie," she tried to hypnotize him.

He scrunched up his face but then relaxed. Another face replaced his.

19

"Good, very good," Wakanda said, "Make the nose a little smaller, the forehead larger. That's good." She was proud of Coyote. At last he was learning to change without his rubber props. The face resembled Kevin Kline, which was good. Wakanda encouraged him, "He played presidents in two other movies, you know."

"What? Presidents? Hmmm. I could be President, later. Good thinking. But first, to the senate seatings."

"But, Coyote, you can't go until the recount, stupid."

"Don't call me stupid!" he said and felt his face, fluffing up his hair. "Nonsense, I'll just be there when they admit I won. I want to go there now!"

Wakanda wondered if this was life imitating art or art imitating art. She sighed and got back in the driver's seat.

Coyote sniffed and got in the back seat to be chauffeured.

Coyote arrived in DC by private car. He started by dancing the Status Dance in the parking lot of Applebys. His staff watched from inside, wondering if they maybe should be paid more, or at least in advance. After a few minutes, they came out and brought Coyote inside to the reserved room.

Coyote sniffed them unobtrusively as they introduced themselves, identifying health, deception and potential mates. He confidently told them of his plans.

"You know, the chances are they will turn you away," replied Brian.

"Not with all my limos, I think. We need to soften up the Senate," Coyote nodded to his own words.

"Automatic weapons?" suggested Jimmy, the security guru.

"No, just an ally or two, and a favorable news report."

"I can arrange those, I think," suggested Glenda, the Press Secretary. "But, first a few rules about public statements: Please wear boxer shorts, do not admit having sex of any kind, do not mangle innocent metaphors, do not be too honest, and do not suggest any illegal activities as taxable resources. Please!"

"Can I get you some miniburger, sliders, or bunglets?" asked a short woman, who had introduced herself as 'Beloved.'

"**What** are you going to do, while you are waiting for the recount?" asked Glenda.

"All the traditional things, Coyote answered. "The 'gaggle' at the White House, the google at the office, the reading of hotline, the eating of the power lunch, the viewing of the news channel, the releasing of news on teevee or if that fails, the Stewart Show, then the planning for fund-raising for the next election, the budget battles, and the recesses—that's my favorite part, I get to go home and mingle with the little people."

"I have your first interview for now. We have been cultivating a reporter at the *Washington Globe*. Are you up to it?"

Coyote gave a thumb's up and was introduced to Courtney Random. "What do you dislike most about Washington?" asked Random.

"Seattle or Spokane?"

"No, DC."

"Obviously, the constant concrete hierarchy, the caste system cemented in place with qwik-set. It's terrible. How can I demonstrate my own power if everyone is more powerful? Think, I am of the lowly trading class, not the scholarly or warrior class."

"But, still, doubtless the farmers or untouchables," noted Random sarcastically.

"I think farmers should have higher and more respect, now that they are fewer and more elite mechanists and chemists," judged Coyote.

"And, the untouchables? The invisibles?"

"No, I see them all the time, running gas stations and speedy marts, but I never ask their opinions."

"Like you do the wise scholars?"

"No, just purchased professional scholars."

"And, if you are not seated?"

"Life is nasty, brutish and short at this stage of political devolution. I will merely return to serving my local constituents as a man of the people."

"Very noble," said Courtney, then struck hard, "There are rumors that you stole a Winnebago, you were implicated in the death of a rancher, and that you stole some candy from a 7/11."

Coyote was nonplussed, "I think we need to remember that 7/11 was a very hard time for all of us, especially those who lived in Pearl Harbor. I am ashamed at the candy bars. Hunger. That was probably true," and Coyote hung his head in sham-shame.

"Thank you Senator-elect Jones for showing the people that shame is not dead, that you can feel and express those feelings as honestly as the low of the lowest of us," she said dryly.

"Untouchables? I think not," C said moistly.

"Well, anyway, you have my thanks," she said cynically.

"Is there possibly another way you could thank me, a way that involved less clothing?"

"What do you mean?" Courtney asked.

"Ah, swimming, perhaps, in the Congressional pool."

"I thought that was a car pool? What are you planning now?"

"I intend to enroll the kids in St. Albans School, to perpetuate the entitlements of my family to power and knick knacks."

"What about the Cabot Lodges and the Kennedys, the Doles and Rockefellers, the Clintons and Gores, the Bushes and Shrubs?"

"These are powerful clans, make no mistake, but even clans are replaced over decades, as they seem to get weaker with every generation, sadly—must be that sacrifice takes something out of the clan—oh, well, they usually get to keep the money."

"But, will you have the power to do things to accomplish good laws?" she asked.

"Not exactly. Anything the people can do, we can undo, just like anything the people deny, we can affirm. Heh, heh."

In the Holiday Inn that night, oddly alone, Coyote basked in his satisfaction at handling the first impressions with dignity and humility. The next morning Coyote met with his people to plan his grand entrance into the city.

"There is a movement to *not* seat you, until the runoff and recount. What do you need?" Brian asked.

"Status distinctions are made by the size of the motorcade. That is why I want more," Coyote answered. "I want 25 cars, 6 motorcycles and 3 helicopters to announce my arrival at the Senate."

"Is that a good idea?"

"Yes, I think so. The more flash I have the less likely I'll be flushed."

It did not work. Officials at the entrance to Congress refused to accept the credentials of Itsayaya Jones of Kansas. They counseled him to wait until after the mandatory recount.

After being barred from the swearing-in ceremony, Jones took his limos and surrounded the building for a few minutes to display his defiant posture and public support.

Jones' lawyers asked the Kansas Supreme Court to compel Governor Tinijoy to sign an election certificate as a final ruling in the race. The day before, they had submitted a brief to the high court of Kansas to throw out the recount challenge of candidate Turtle.

Coyote was disappointed, but he knew that blind persistence paid off. He addressed his people, although four or five seemed to be missing. "We absolutely have to get to work. The first thing is to make appointments at the White house every week, maybe Camp David a few times, and the President's Chicago Condo right away. I need a certificate and a photo showing me on Air Force One. Then leak that to the press.

I'll need new clothes. See if you can find the Senate Goodwill store, so the clothes can be expensive, yet rumpled and slightly worn. Sharp, yet aged and intubated imbued with power. Set up a manicure appointment. I'll need to see a plastic surgeon—"

"About what?" Brian asked.

"Maybe add a small jowl, grey hair in front of my ears," Coyote nodded.

"You might want to get those surgically reduced, ha ha?" offered Brian.

"What do you mean?"

"Never mind."

"I'll need a raspberry to keep messages on and to receive praise from my constituents."

"Blackberry?" asked Glenda.

"If that's a more politically correct color, then yes. I'll need an invitation from the Cosmos Club. Just tell them I've seen a lot of it."

"What?" Glenda asked.

"The cosmos, of course. Oh, and I'll need a Nobel Prize for Peace or maybe just a suitable academic title from the Hornblower Institute for Advanced Studies, something like 'Scholar of Peace Studies.' Or, from the American Fantasizing Institute? Ambassador Bolting would know.

"Will you need a plaque or certificate?"

"Whatever. Backdate it to the Clinton era. "

Cameras & Sirens

"What do you want me to do, sir?" asked Wilma, a go-for.

"You have the most important job. Follow the camera. If there's a camera, I want to be centered in it. If it has audio, I want to be filling it."

"With what, sir, you don't have any positions yet," said Wilma bravely.

"Nor do I want to. They are very limiting. I can speak without a position. I'll just start with my family history, my grandpa, Limpy, and his father, the sun. Then my friendships with famous people. Not just famous, but top-drawer. And athletes as well, and movie stars. Why I was one of the last to see Marilyn Monroe alive; it was, well, the garbage can was open and—"

"Sir, a camera!"

It was a false alarm, just a seven-year-old with a videocam.
Glenda was correcting him on his solipsistic egoism, "There is no 'I' in team."

"So what, there is no 'p' or 'q' either. There is no 'I' in Coyote. I mean there is an 'I' in Itsayaya Jones, but I want to be in the company of other vowels and consonants. That is why I say I so much. My view is more important. I mean of course if the people say it is, with votes and gifts, of course."

"The people have expressed concern that your attention span is too short. What do you have to say to that?"

"I think it is longer than most—of course my nose and other body parts are longer—length is an important measure of success. I certainly want to pay attention to those things that require—hey, look, a fire truck, but no sirens. You know the words siren comes from the Greek for—"

"Thank you, sir, I think that—"

"There goes the siren. Wrong address maybe, or got worse."

"Obviously, I need power mongers and money brokers," Coyote was saying to his shrinking team. "I need those people to prop me up when the media discovers I have no substance, nor want any. I know that is not an attractive characteristic of a senator, or of any human being, but I need the power. Let's get it the hi-power way, by attracting other powers and promising to give them a slice of the rewards of further power."

"I think a deal is close," said Brian smugly. "We can negotiate, especially on the reputation of your opponent. Also, Jimmy Carter can call and say what a good congressman you will make, when you're in the congress.

And, don't forget, we will continue the media strategy and have coverage everywhere saying the law is on your side. And, we'll keep praising everyone for doing their job, even those who are not, of course, since they might be important medially-speaking."

"What's the worst?"

"Drama fatigue. Everyone gets tired." Brian nodded off.

Coyote had his first television interview on the Linda Meadows show.

"What are you? A democrat?" she asked directly.

"Officially, but actually a Repubacrat or Democan. Obviously not a democant or repubicat, ha ha. Seriously, I accepted the talking points of the Dem party, as well as the fund raisers and rallies. I am loyal, as long as I am bought, but I can't be bought for less than 6 times what I cost originally. That is loyalty you cannot buy, well, I mean afford, realistically, so I am loyal in a pragmatic, a very American, pragmatic way."

"You're about to make a statement on evolution and politics," Linda predicted.

"Let me qualify that part about evolution. It is about survival of the fittest, but kin-selection lets the fittest kin and its members survive, and that is true of cultures, which is why the English Australian culture changed faster than the Aboriginal culture. It was more fitter, more kinny. My family, my people, made sacrifices to get me in office. I have to pay back those sacrifices by getting them jobs in Washington."

"But, that's as bad as your opponent."

"I feel for my opponent, whose relatives were trapped in the tar pits of California and who has proven to be less fit as a politician." Politicians told lies, so it was already fiction, and Coyote was as fictitious as any. He was satisfied with his performance.

Linda continued, "Do you have a position on Iraq?"

"Of course, I am located 4500 miles west of it. There, see, I have a sense of humor. But seriously, Iraq has many problems that we can solve with new campaigns. For instance, smoking; we need an anti-smoking campaign there badly. People are smoking too much and too much of the wrong things. And expiration dates on milk cartons or water bottles. It is impossible to get reliable information on the freshness on drinks. That would make people happier right there.

Car safety is another big issue; seat belts are just not being used, although if the car blows up, it might be better to exit without being restrained by a burning nylon belt."

"And, Afghanistan, it is still in turmoil. What would you do?" Linda asked finally getting to the marrow.

"Obviously, I'd start with the turbans. The designs are old and predictable. I think a Minister of Turban Design could quiet things down. I think we should encourage the market system. People are on the right track with opium. Entrepreneurs need to be able to grow it, without being afraid of being bombed. Of course, we could never legalize it or import it in this country, but we could broker a deal with the Chinese and force them to import and use it to keep their people happy, now that they have less food to eat and more pollution to avoid. You see, Tina, there are things that a good leader, someone like me, of course, could suggest to further the concerns of world peace in other countries."

"Linda! And, the violence in the United States?"

"Tax it. Simply put a tax on every act of violence. The Masai have the right idea—and who doesn't admire that culture?—whenever you hurt, rape or kill someone, you pay a penalty of fifteen sheep or two cattle or something. You don't make laws against violence or promote some other namby-pamby kind of goody-twoshoes ethical actions, you just tax it. Why, the government would get enough money from domestic fights alone to support Social Security and Medicare for ninety more years. Violence will happen anyway. Don't put people in prisons. Let them be productive members of society and just pay a few taxes for their proclivities. Please, it's the capitalist way, and we know capitalism is the winner. Let's go all the way, or risk being un-American. You like America, don't you, Mindy? Don't you?"

"Linda. Unquestionably, but others may question soon-to-be senator I. Jones ideas on foreign and domestic policies. Next up is former commentator Newt Gingerich and his wife Salamandra Juice Newton. Jim, what do you have for us?"

Coyote bowed gracefully and left to his next triumphal exposure, loosening his yellow tie and black buttons.

On the Stewart Show, with Herman Daily, Coyote admitted to being soft on Bush, "Those who do the nation's business should not be shackled by bad rules and accountability. They are too busy. That is why I backed Bush on every issue, from frumious invasions to torture methods and excessive vacation schedules. I appreciated the leadership. The good lord told him what was best for the country, what with the coming apocalypse and all. His energy and drive—that was supported by his monthly vacations. His assurance and direction—that was supported by words from some bible or other. No one could exceed him in patriotism or obliviousness, that is obvious."

"Even after it became obvious that the country was being damaged?" asked Herman Daily.

"The country was damaged by the greed of a few, not by the leaders."

"The few were given the country on a platter, by those leaders," Daily nailed.

"I wasn't a leader at that time, which is why I want to lead now. There is still a profit to be made or a bubble to be inflated for profit. That is capitalism. People do not have be forced to invest in ponzi things or bubbles. They do it out of consuming greed. No animal, except for Grasshopper, would be so stupid to put all its seeds in one hole."

"Grasshopper?" asked Herman.

"Yes, master, I am ready. Brand my forearms with the hot, heavy metal of accomplishment."

"Brand?"

"Yes, always trust a brand. It means something."

"Damage?"

"If you say so. Goodbye. I hope I shed some light on this."

"Itsayaya Jones, candidate for office." Daily sighed and hung his head.

'**Candidate** Jones is facing legal action by the Kansas legislature for allegedly stuffing the ballot boxes in two counties,' said a person speaking under the condition of anonymity.

Jones answered in a terse statement that this was a matter of integrity of the representatives of the people of that fine state.

Turtle stated to his loyal supporters, "This is simply Jones thumbing his nose at the citizens of Kansas, as well as at the US Government and the entire world, and yeah, the animal nations."

In Kansas, Fox was explaining the concepts of human government to Otter and Badger: "The tribe that runs the government is a kinship system like that of foragers. But, the game is money, that is, symbols. The system has its own mythology. It has its own cultural norms. There are hunters and warriors, shaman and nurturers. They have special rituals and festivals, fertility rites and passages. There is human sacrifice to keep the rest healthy. It is a tragedy, so there is a chorus to tell us what we need to know."

"Kinship is first, rituals R us!" they chanted.

"Not now! I'll say when," advised Fox. "*Homo sapiens politicus*. Remember that subspecies. He strives for power for the sake of power, not for kick-backs or blowjobs, not for face-time or monuments. Those things may be vehicles, but not the real meaningful goal. And the power has no goals to be achieved. It only exists to be exercised, like a Bow flux or Ab scrounger fitness tool.

"The subspecies *sapiens politicus* is captive to primitive rituals older than democracy and to bizarre motions more basic than helping one's self to the possessions of others. What kind of culture could have developed this strange mutation? Agriculture is the guilty party. It produced too much surplus, and someone had to claim the right to it, to justify begging the gods for it. That someone became the first politician and the first king. Then, that surplus became a permanent entitlement for the mutant politician. And, that led to a new subspecies.

"A new subspecies!" they chorused.

"Not yet! There is a charm in someone who charms others to get, flaunt, and misuse power for the silliest reasons. And the charmed are surely protected from rational behavior or judgment."

"So, do you think I could run for office? For this Agriculture party?" Badger asked, brushing dirt off his nose.

Otter regarded Fox, and then asked, "We can still play, can't we? I mean we don't use symbols. We are symbols, aren't we?"

Fox looked at Otter, who rolled on his back; then he looked at Badger, who was looking at him. He decided to start over, "Look, when your mother made you leave the den and look for your own food, that was like government ..."

But, Badger curled up and went to sleep by Otter.

"They sleep," whispered the chorus.

Fox shrugged and went to look for lunch.

Tried Convicted Celebrated Deified OR *Judge Jimmy Jams Jams*

Coyote had to answer the door himself; his staff seemed to have all gone on other missions. Agent James Black asked him to turn around and present his wrists. Coyote said that would do no good as his wrists would still be in front of him, so how could Black reach them.

Black said "Put your hands behind your back." Coyote did that as he turned but his hands were still on the other side of his body. Agent Charles Brown walked around and cuffed Coyote gently, saying, "I like your stand on law enforcement."

Coyote was taken to a public location for questioning. He was made to listen to tapes where Badger and Otter confessed to ramming in extra votes at polling places.

They tried to get Coyote to confess to planning the entire crime. They softened him up by accusing him of many related illegalities.

"I was never guilty of a *fonzi* scheme!" protested Coyote. "It was an innocent investment in old day-time TV shows. Totally innocent, as innocent as the shows themselves!"

Badger was brought in to talk to Coyote. He was wearing a brown T-shirt that said '*The simple life* den-cleaning service.'

"Why are you helping humans?" Coyote asked.

Badger replied: "Because they have control and power. They have converted everything. There are fewer animals now. Who am I going to work for? It's just economics and I want to survive."

"Oh, great," Coyote muttered, now all the animals were competing with him to get human wealth and cars and stuff. Coyote was released on his own recognizance, pending trial. He noted that he made the *NY Times'* List of Terrible Deeds.

Coyote knew he had to do something drastic. He convinced Beloved to come back and release a series of apologies to try to shore up the old reputation, but they seemed to be endless.

Part 1, on the *Yesterday Show*. "I gave a poor choice of words. I meant to say that my opponent Turtle was like an onion, not a bomb, so complex with layers of deepness, each stronger and more odiferous than the outer."

Part 2, on the *Today Show*. "I apologize. There is nothing more I can say. I slandered an honest man for political gain. I have no excuse for my inexcusable transgression. I mean I have been working too hard for the people, and maybe I said those things from exhaustion."

Part 3, on the *Tomorrow Show*. "Please forgive me, as I learn from my own mistakes. My words were totally unacceptable and I apologize.

for them. I was broken down by the responsibilities of office and family. I was just winging it because you expected me to say something about it."

Part 4, on the *Everyday Show*. "Oh, God, I'm so sorry. I only hope you can find it in your hearts, noble and generous hearts they are, to forgive me for me deeply grievous error. I ate Turtle's family. I will apologize in any venue on any forum for any reason for that crime. My staff is researching reasons now. Black Entertainment Television and Chinese People's Camera have agreed to give me the public flailing I need for my wicked, wicked stupidity. I am so sorry that this was recorded and was made visible to all of you. The media just has no sense or judgment about context and intent."

Amy Cooter, at the *Everyday Show* summed it up, "What is Coyote? He is engaged in deception, using flattery, slander, and sycophancy. He is corrupt, emotionally and financially. He conspires with foreign powers to undermine the independence of animals. He embroils us all in battles to serve his own ends. He is shameless and sexually depraved, a threat to the health of our children. He is simply vulgar and degraded."

Coyote tried to reverse that for his enemies: "I am reluctant to stand before you to speak of myself, but I have been slandered and animals may draw rash conclusions. Not flattery or deception, it is a risk to me to speak forwardly, frankly and honestly. My assistance and advice can lead to success and prosperity. Look at all I have done for you, conferred on you." Pretty much everyone commented on his incoherence.

That did not work. And Coyote was held for trial, which was rapid for Washington or television standards.

Judge Jams asked Coyote if he had a statement to make.

"But, your honor, it's not my fault. It is just evolution. I was made to change to adapt by being more violent and killing more for dinner. Coyote was a man in time and a stage of evolution, All the worlds a stage in evolution. Coyote himself is a snake with legs and a talker. I know that I have a dark side now, and I embrace it. The real danger is people like you, Your Horror, who refuse to believe that you have a dark side. And that your dark side leads to homelessness, violence, rape, poverty and selfish thoughts. Mine just leads to weak jokes and random humor—or ingestion."

That did not work. Coyote was sentenced to the Federal Executive Corrective Farm outside Maryland. Although he moaned and apologized, he rejoiced inwardly to be surrounded by wire and fences, all of which rested on good farm soil.

It took Coyote a week to dig his way out, and another week to get back to Kansas. He was careful to keep to his animal shape as much as possible, although his new Bill Clinton mask was useful for getting some free food at restaurants by highways. He was an animal again!

Reamble: I have a Nightmare

Coyote knew that he had to clear up the misunderstandings. He had to make things right. At radio station KURG on Powhattan, he made a tape with Fox on camera. Fox had written the words, also, borrowed from a famous man of peace. Coyote regarded his audience of one and spoke eloquently: "I have a nightmare! I have a nightmare that animals will be sucked into the vortex of human decline—look at beaver, for instance, who doesn't bother building a dam and a lodge anymore, just nibbling off the bottom of a Wal-Mart playhouse and moved it to the center of a puddle. That's sad. Even as we revel in advances in technology games and luxury, I still have a nightmare!

I have a nightmare that animals will adopt to the industrial playgrounds leaving behind their forests and swamps, and the clever things they make and need.

I have a nightmare, that nothing we do will stop the mad rush to destruction, that nothing they do will deter others, more powerful, from destroying everything.

I have a nightmare that the earth cannot recover from the constant interference with its cycles and down-draining the very process and capacity of renewal.

I have a nightmare that we will make a desert planet too hot for any desert creature, and this from the image of the human desire for simplicity, the simplicity of extinction.

I have a nightmare that this speech will go on too long, that you all will skip to the next page, but—

This nightmare cannot be avoided. It cannot be denied or explained away. It cannot be outgrown by economics or tempered by politics. It is the nightmare of tragedy—of good actions taken and turned by fate into a trap. It is a nightmare of surprise change and violent destructive catastrophes.

But, it is a nightmare that can be changed, moderated, anticipated and ameliorated through preparation. The nightmare can be learned from, it can be strategized and held, softened and weakened, stroked and kissed—"

And Coyote went on, explaining how politicians like him could make things better.

But, then he ruined it with words from his sponsor, "That is why I take '*Deepflox 770*' at night before bed; it lets me sleep without nightmares. This fine product from Density Labs will let you, too, sleep innocently and safely. It is nonaddictive and reasonably priced. Remember, 'Deepflox 770' at the corner drug store."

Knowing he was going to have to flee for his life, Coyote made another tape for his future pups. He faced the camera and taped the tobacco from his pipe.

After a long, unnecessary rambling introduction recanting his recent history, he said, "I have been disgraced by others for my efforts to make the world a better place, a dream rather than a nightmare. So, I am going into exile. I want you to tell you, my future pups, if I am not there to train you myself, to carry yourselves proudly, drag your tail low, not high like those silly captive dogs. You are carnivores; others are prey. You have the entitlement to make the world a tastier place by eating the old and young, the slow and stupid. Remember your heritage as survivors, as animals, as coyotes. Now go hunting!"

In his hide-out den southeast of Powhattan, Coyote was ruminating on the lessons he had learned:

Never admit anything to anyone, in case there was tape or video. Never underestimate the roles of cruelty, stupidity and status as reasons for cultural behaviors, e.g., ceremonies to impress the poor.

Never go against the self-interests of a voter, or ask them to inconvenience themselves, even to save the planet.

And, never, ever, trust the Media to be fair or unbiased.

However, he did see his 'nightmare' speech on teevee at a bar in Horton at 3 a.m. It did not wake the drunks.

Part 2. Gambles

Army Time Avatar Space Coyote Energy Zero Mass

How long a time had it been? Coyote's dreams changed—from an orange snake, he was compressed into a small grey cube. Nothing happened for a long time, then he was flattened, electrified and linked with others. He expanded and reconnected. He could feel so much happening. He was a full Coyote again, restored, but *orange*—but where was he? It didn't seem real. He was trapped somehow. He could do some things, like think and breath, but he could only walk on certain narrow paths, with certain energies. He had to follow some rules.

Digital-Coyote did not eat, exactly, since he was a blue avatar, but he set up games and hunted mice through a subterranean maze, keeping score. One day, he was shocked when an orange coyote appeared in the maze, also hunting mice. He shouted: "Hey, you, this is a one-person game!"

"Who says? Who are you? Why are you blue?"

"I'm a resident here, part of the Mars project. How did you get in? Why are you orange?"

"I have always lived here, although I can't remember much. I think I am, I am Coyote," the intruder said.

"Well, some kind of coyote. Do we have a template or something? I mean, you look an awful lot like me, except for that bumper-car color."

"How would I know? I have always been, well, actually I think I was a snake for a long time. Then I woke up and I was in this track with you."

"A snake. That's wild. All I know is that you had to come in with the new batch of chips."

"But, how was I born?" Orange Coyote asked.

"That's a tough question. Maybe you're Chemical-Coyote or Chip-Coyote. Me, I was created to be an avatar in a military computer, but my template was killed, blinked out like a cheap bulb, although I continue to shine. I must be immortal. Maybe you are, too."

"That would be nice. Can we get out of here?"

"I'll call you C-Coyote until we figure you out."

"What shall I call you?"

"Digital Coyote, or D-coy."

D-Coy meditated: Questions arise when life and machines merge. Technology accelerates, molecular robots spread through recesses of all matter, making rocks and clouds into living computers. Nanobots may not have the same goals as life or avatars. They could convert the planet biomass to itself in months. No track record, no prediction, D-Coy feared.

Three on a Match

Eventually, D-Coyote and C-Coyote decide to meet Flesh Coyote, F-Coyote. They sent him a ticket to Kansas City, where they could invade a large enough computer. They promised him power, money and mice.

Coyote sneaked to the Universal Insurance Company and was cleared and taken to the Information Technology Center. A sudden, external shutdown emptied the floor of all human presence. D-Coy was pleased with his manipulations, as he heard Flesh Coyote ask a question.

"So, you're an 'afterthought'?" Coyote asked.

"No, an Astronaut," corrected D-Coyote, thinking 'your brain is like an empty bedpan.'

"You know," Coyote started, "I always wanted to go to the moon, especially after Hummingbird said it was possible. I don't understand any of this," he admitted, "you're planning to go to Mars?"

D-Coyote said, "Let's go back to when you had me made as an avatar for the computer, M1L1E."

"What is an avatar again?" asked Coyote.

D-Coy began slowly, "An avatar, what I am, is a digital character who can wander around complex 3-D environments testing and probing them, talking to other avatars, testing and probing them—"

"Sex?" Coyote asked.

"Sure, exactly."

"Simulated?" Coyote was thinking about his future cash cow, the National Pornographic. What could he use for it to make more money, avatars having sex?

"Not to me. It's real."

"How real can that be?" Coyote asked, then jumped as the chair he was leaning on gave him an electric shock.

"Was that real? You bet. I just sent a signal, which triggered a short and let you have some of my electricity, so don't give me any real distinctions shit."

"Okay, okay. So, what do you do in there?"

"I explore Mars."

"Really, doesn't seem like much."

"It is. I can feel the wind. I can feel the windblown dust and walk through it as it piles in soft dunes like small snowdrifts. I can smell—"

"Why are you there? Vacation?"

"No, work—don't ask. One of my jobs is to understand the visual distortion from living in a light atmosphere. Perception is a problem like on the Moon. Astronauts underestimate distances. Then, the dust causes serious backscattering of light—"

"I've done some serious backscattering myself," Coyote pulled his tail and farted. Then snickered.

"And, I have some specific projects, such as testing these new gloves," and D-Coyote held up two hands, one with a white glove, the other with a yellow.

"How can you do that? You're a Coyote and have feet."

"No mean feat either. I am, of course, as flexible as you, and just appear like you in my natural state. But. I can rearrange almost everything. Hey, before we talk more, I need you to meet somebody," D-Coyote acted all mysterious and so.

An orange form materialized from the Marscape. "This is C-Coyote. He is a chemical form that emerged from a substrate chip. I call him Chippy."

"Hey, a little dignity here. I am the real Coyote. I was killed by Seth, but brought back to life—"

"By Fox?" Coyote asked.

"No, it was another strange process, self-assembly from a chemical pattern, as D-Coyote explained it to me."

"I am the real original Coyote here," Coyote boasted, "I demand you help me get elected!"

"You are kind of like my primitive remote ancestor," D-Coyote said. "Say, listen, we need to give you a name, so we can tell each other apart. I'll call you O-Coyote since you are trapped in the organic medium."

"No!" said Coyote, "I am Coyote."

"Flesh Coyote?"

"No!"

"How about A-Coyote, then?" suggested C-Coyote. "You're Analog. That way, you'll be first among us, alphabetically-speaking."

"Hmmm," meditated Coyote, too slowly.

"Excellent!" agreed D-Coyote, "We are D, C, A. Sounds better than C, O, D anyway."

"A, D, C! Last offer. Listen," started Coyote or A-Coyote, "I'd love to shoot the breeze with you constructs, but I have to defend myself and my home from —

"The military?" asked C-Coyote.

"Ah, yeah, partly."

"We need to show you a couple of things," said D-Coyote. "Sit down in that chair and look at the monitor. I'm going to leave my hologram here, but I need to be online to show you."

The flat screen in front of Coyote flashed dark and light. D-Coyote was there. "Pay attention now, O'Coy—hey, are you Irish? Or just Organic?—I mean A-Coy. Complicated." He sat and scratched a flea.

Coyote noticed, with his finely tuned senses. "Why did you do that? Did you scratch a tick or flea?"

D-Coy looked thoughtful. "I guess it's just a behavior of the model. Not important."

Coyote asked quickly, "A physiological expression of mood?"

D-Coy frowned, plainly not wanting to discuss this. "No, my body does not feel anything like an itch. I have no musculoskeletal frame driven by hormonal chemicals. It's more like an associated logical structure of thinking."

"You think?" asked Coyote.

"Yes, I modify patterns of interlocking variables in response to external and really exprogrammic stimuli."

"Not thinking at all!" crowed Coyote.

"Yes, it's like you do. We are exchanging data only in 'words' for your convenience. I could switch to smells or numbers. C-Coy and I can rechannel bit streams directly to each other. No old filters like your big ears or nose. I can have any nose I want. Look!" and the image had a nose two feet long.

"Hey, can you do that with your penis? Never mind. What's that like, the data thing?" Coyote asked, despite himself curiosity winning again.

"It's a direct and full spectrum," C-Coy answered, "Imagine you're in a forest but can see only pine trees, but you know it's a forest so you do not look for more or see much more. For us, the forest is filled with many other trees connected through the roots and air, animals, plants, fungus, bacteria, viruses, hundreds of players."

"Wow, can I get in?"

"Sorry, but we are you and are already in, but if you look at the monitor I can show you a sample."

"Three would be too many," C-Coy whispered under his 'breath,' glad he did not tell D-coy about his experiment with a reverse avatar of himself. When the time was right, he would transfer to his creation. He was distracted by a strange sight: A brown coyote sitting in a chair next to holograms of a blue coyote and an orange one, all watching a large screen with the blue and orange coyotes on Mars, showing a glowing image of a rainforest.

Coyote was leaving when D-Coy gave him a wrist computer, "For contacting us for help."

"Me, need help?" Coyote smirked. "Oh, by the way, I want to be known as Coyote Prime."

Flashback OR *Billboard Tropical Flesh*

Woodchuck had his head at burrow-level, looking for any predators. His eyes, ears and nose were near the top of his head and suited for caution. His long whiskers and large nose were also useful for sensing danger, as well as for finding food. He ducked back down, using his long claws and strong feet to dig further south. His chisely front teeth let him eat the hard roots of shrubs. His small ears tucked in and kept out loose dirt. He was just starting to add extra body fat and thicker fur to keep warm in the winter.

As he started his new burrow, Badger was watching Coyote. Coyote caught a Groundhog and ate a bite, then he raced across the field, caught Woodchuck and took a bite. Then he raced back and had another bite of the Groundhog.

"What are you doing?" Badger asked.

Coyote snapped, "Isn't it obvious? I'm having ground chuck."

Badger shook his head and decided to take a nap.

That night, Coyote was walking along, thinking about his strange avatars. The night was cool and windless. There was no moon. *Whaamuf*—he was being ripped apart! His bones started to thicken, especially the legs. He grew taller. His canines curved over his lips. His larger eyes collected more of the spectrum. His pelt thickened and grew out producing a gentle, multicolored glow. It had happened again. The genes had been triggered by something. Coyote felt powerful. He started running towards the blue glow of a track of mouse urine that lead to a hole. His front claws tapped ominously as he ran. He reached the hole and excavated it with a scoop, then downed the mouse.

He had to think. He knew from the last time that he would run out of energy unless he was careful. The backup photosynthesis was worthless at night. He had to save his energy, and he had to get to Doctor Splicer. He lay down and looked over his magnificent body, dire wolf, tropical fish, oak leaf, Kestrel eyes, and horse penis. He went to sleep.

The next morning he was normal. And, he was normal the next day and the next night. Late that night, after a time at the Powhattan Bar and Grill, he pulled over to piss. He lifted his leg—too much Captain Morgan. At least he knew why the other customers stood like that. Made pissing easier.

It was a quiet moonless night. Cool, windless. He took a bite of his doughnut, thoughtfully liberated from a police car in front of the bar. Then he felt the change slowly, as his bones became denser. Just as he started to move, he fell asleep.

The next morning he was normal again. This was ridiculous! Spicer had said the environment was the trigger, but how could he control the environment? He wanted control of his flesh. Everything was flesh. Coyote was flesh, mouse, grass, light were flesh. Coyote had to experience everything. That was why he existed. But, he had to get control. He had to get to Splicer. Maybe a few mice first.

Alteramble: *Fox Gives Up* OR *Paper Wasps*

Coyote forgot what was so important that he was traveling to Topeka, but then he saw Fox, "Hey, Fox, what's your killometer reading?"

"What? Dunno. Stopped counting. Killing humans made no difference, they just bred faster."

"Ha, yea, ha ha, sort of like, ummm—"

"Coyotes?"

"Ah, no, we are just naturally productive. I was going to say flies."

Fox announced: "I understand humanity much better now. They are a paper-making species, like paper wasps."

"Paper wasps," chimed a Chorus offstage.

"Stop that!" demanded Fox, "This is not a Tragedy, it is a Farce."

Coyote looked around for the source of the voices, then replied, "So, what made them that way?"

"They hate trees. A species thing, maybe from a history of leopards jumping from trees and eating them. This is their revenge, cutting trees for paper. Won't be happy until the planet is treeless."

"That's kind of harsh."

"So, I've decided not to extinguish them, or destroy them, just make them into animals again."

"How?" asked Coyote.

"By trapping them in their toys."

"How?"

"Glad you asked. My strategy is: Get humans involved in machines and lock them in. Hyperconnect them in a mobile, wireless society. Keep them involved with the user interface between laptop, electric car and house. They can use avatars as representatives in a virtual world. They can rework their identities and relationships in electron space, on virtual pathways to explore the future. Control and design are totalitarian in a virtual world with oppression and censorship, but they won't care, because they will think they have control, at last."

"Sounds brilliant," said Coyote, "but, can't we just admit that autos were a bad decision and drove us in the wrong direction?"

"No, not radical enough."

"Less radical than eating them? I thought you were a herbivore, you only ate people named Herb?"

"No more than you are a carnivore who only eats carnies. Hey, I have a message from Wakanda. Wants you to meet her at the Song contest tonight."

"Oh, great," said Coyote. "I used to win every Song contest, when they were just howling. Now, I can't keep up."

Am. I-dull OR *Soft Rock Blue Croon*

"Hear that singer, Da-rule?" asked Wakanda.

"Drool? No thanks."

"Coyote, he's a famous rapper. He's appearing on the final segment of Am I-dull."

"So, who is *this* guy?" Coyote asked, pointing to a cowboy hat extruding a human body.

"That skol-dipping, Jack-swiggin, cancer-generating, boredom-crushing nightmare is country singer Bosco Brentworth. Listen," urged Wakanda, "It's from his new hit record."

Bosco smoothed his beard and started his song:

"You were dipping Mike, while I was dipping Skol
Yea, you were fixing Mark while I was fixing trucks.
After all I've done, all I suffered, the hurts still linger
Why, when I gave you the ring, you gave me the finger."

Coyote thought the guitar was weak without the amplified words. He could not see why Wakanda was interested in human howling. Also, he was sure the next singer Randy Pebbles was Fox in disguise, since Fox only had two masks, with the same red face.

Randy started singing:

"Give me more, oh, give me more of that terrifying horrible war
Roll me over, I'm a whore, for that terrible deadly war.
Give me security, give me order, and I'll give up my body for
The boredom of heaven or—"

Coyote tuned out and started to stroke Wakanda's haunch, but she brushed his paw away and hushed him.

Someone else had claimed the microphone, some hyper tenor:

"You can have my headdress with its flashy brain
and you can have my body with its sexual buzz
Oh, you can have my craving and its yellow stain
But you can't take my mojo, or I'll call the fuzz."

Then it was Martin Caust and his Big Tuba. Not just big, jazz tuba, but a mash-up of funk, hip-hop, and tub-wub. Martin introduced himself:

"I was a band-leader at 2, the road shows were my schooling.
It's a horn! The tuba. Get it? Horn means jazz, horn means sex,
And now, let's undress and go:

Oh, baby, baby (tooot tooot) I love you, ho!
Can't wait to kiss you gently, beyatch!
We spoon under the moon in June (toot)
Then I get my arms around your skanky ass—"

Coyote left to get ready for his turn. Then, he was doing his best to sound like Mel Gourmet channeled by Snoopy Dogbert Dog:

"Oh, baby, baby, baby, I love your big 'b's!
Your lobes they comfort me in matters of philosophy.
No, no, I do not joke. Post hoc ergo propter hoc
is not a threat to those who know logical fallacy.
Yes, more than 'a's or 'c's, I just love your big 'b's,
Plump, grey and wrinkled—their surface area
makes our life together an intellectual circus
and we both swing as from a trapeze
on constructs of words with ease.
Baby, baby, baby, baby, I love your big brains!
B, b, b, b, b! Unh, unh, unhuh, unhuh! Huunh!"

Coyote almost had the crowd with his sensual 'Unhs' but he ruined it at the last minute by urinating on the stage.

"I could have won," he said later. "I just had too much Captain Morgan while I was waiting. Listen, I was just thinking of my next song:

"I got rhythm, you hear monotony.
I got melody, you feel the turmoil
Yea, I got harmony, you get headaches
I got music, you just feel sick dah lah de dah."

Bosco walked away with the trophy, surrounded with a bevy of trophy bitches who clutched at his puffy sleeves.

Alteramble: Coyote bacter

Again, for the millionth time, Coyote was depressed. How could he lose a contest to be an idol? He was unique in his voice and range.

He was lying on the forest floor shouting for Fungus, "Mike, are you there?"

Then there was a faint answer, "Mike dried up, nothing left."

"Who are you?" Coyote asked.

"Stephanie Bacteria," came the answer.

"How can you talk to me?"

"Good question, shows you think critically. The answer is shocking to you, I'll bet. Everything thinks. Turns out that DNA is an excellent computer."

"What, you mean even viruses?"

"Shhhhh! You'll wake her up. Just take my word for it. Where was I? Oh, yea, strands link in ways that can communicate, model, or compute."

"What does it compute?"

"History, what's happened, what works under what conditions."

"But, why?"

"Everything computes. Everything exists and it has to know its place. Atoms, molecules, especially large ones like DNA."

"Do I have one? Can I use it?" Coyote asked.

"If you are conscious of it, sure. It's part of your brain anyway, part of your body, your mass."

"Wow. I never thought."

"Oh, ha, you are always thinking."

"How long have you—I mean old are you?"

"Has to be three billion years this week."

"So, Ms. Bacteria, what makes you so durable and strong?"

"Hey, I can take temperatures up to 211 without wilting."

"Shouldn't you be in Centigrade?"

"I've been in Belgrade. If I was in an advanced country like Bulgaria I'd be in centigrade. I can go without water for decades. I survive under rocks at high pressure."

"How could I become like you?" Coyote asked.

"You already are one with me. I live in you. It's warm and constant, except for once every 2-3 months, when you die for a while. I live on, though."

"What can you teach me about life?" Coyote asked, always looking for an edge.

Stephanie started whispering and Coyote had to put his ear to the soil, nodding, getting dirt on his whiskers.

Coyote nodded and said, "So, if I just stay in water, I can—"

Porn for Peace

Coyote coughed up a storm of smoke as he drew on the white pipe, trying to get warm after living in a pond for two days, trying to ingest bacteria and grow wise.

Wakanda looked at the round saucer with a bowl on top; she noted the seven stem holes in the lower body.

Only one was filled and Coyote was using just one made of elm tree wood.

She said, suddenly loud, "You stole that from the Cherokee!"

"Cough, ufff, che che, no, just borrowed it to irritate Eagle."

"For 400 years?"

"There's no time limit on borrowing. Is there?"

"Just common sense, maybe a twentieth of a generation. That was the pipe of peace. Without it, anger has replaced calm thinking."

"It wasn't anger at me, just at a few Delaware."

"They had to give up everything and walk the trail."

"So? I've had to walk some trails. I am sure that the point of this story is clear. This is an undoubtedly true story. If you could just get to it."

Wakanda left, too angry to speak about the trails of suffering left by Coyote's greed and selfishness.

Coyote didn't notice. He had turned to the computer and was playing with his business. The demand for downgraded kinds of art, from pornography to exhibition, was growing. Was art a crime? No. Maybe art was a crime if it included other expressions of art, by force, into a new work. But, how can you force words and patterns to do what they don't want? You can't. So he was clear, morally speaking.

The porn site was doing well, but the feds were tying to tax it more effectively. Fractal pornography was very popular with mathematicians and farmers with jagged edges. A few lawyers visited, but rarely spent more than $50. The ecologists with a taste for theoretical bestiality kept trying to play without paying. Coyote decided to make it a nonprofit corporation for education. That way he could keep his salary of $400,000 a year and donate $300,000 back to the corp.

Coyote was always looking for hooks for his porn empire. Recently he saw one on television that he could use. Some poor Neanderthal in horn rim glasses saw an insurance ad so 'simple' a troglodyte could do it. He threw off his glasses, tore off his shirt and ran down the rain-glistening street. Coyote realized that could be a gripping lead-in to real-life porn situations. As the Neanderthal tore off the rest of his clothes, he could grab a street woman or two, take them back to his cave and have sex with them, in cave-man ways.

He could work in other television themes, from commercials for Viagra to the Horny Housewives of Heartland. And, there might be vast opportunities with geographic and travel channels to combine people's interests in the exotic and the erotic.

On the fractal porn website, Coyote launched his new ezine, not a playhouse or penthouse, but *National Pornographic*, to explore the scientific and geographical differences of sex.

He even had a special section on predictions, under the name Coyostradamus, predictions such as: 'Things will get worse,' 'There will be a great release of gas, then suffering, sneezing, wheezing, suffocating, and people will bemoan their fate,' 'If a man with hair the color of dragon blood and the moustache of an idiot shall trade the short tooth of sweets for the long tooth of metal to steal more honey, then he will have power over females and a sweet disease,' And, 'When half of humanity trades the vacuous idiocy of villages for the stuffed idiocy of cities, and when half the planet is dead, then the entire planet will be consumed with use and turned into highways, parking lots and plastic vistas—and then we can rollerblade and drive forever!'

There was a column on postdictions, which were especially popular: "The housing bubble will collapse in 2008,' 'A politician with charismatic hair will be found guilty of stealing in 2009,' and 'An athlete with skin the color of syrup will be revealed to be cheating on his spouse on 24 November 2009 at 9:48 a.m. EST.' Those were all perfect, of course, referring to the past.

On the same page was an ad for another company Coyote owned. It showed a photo of a house covered with Bubble Wrap. 'Buy some today! Protect your house from the dangerous creeping blown up bubble! Values guaranteed to last over a week longer!'

Contributors would be assigning 10 percent of their subscription to charitable causes, such as blow-up sex-dolls for poor farmers in Indonesia.

Not All are Equal Or I got Mine Why Not You?

Now that he was rich, Coyote became fascinated with poor people and their cute little ways of coping with leftovers and trickledowns.

To be invisible in the city, to execute his research as a neutral observer, Coyote the anthropologist had learned to roll in the dirt and lay on the bench like a homeless person. No one looked directly at him, except other homeless. He could hear what the people had to say and follow them discretely. He knew that disguise was the secret of successful anthropology.

Coyote followed one loser home from the Copper Kitchen where he worked. He had to trot to keep up with the wobbly bicycle. He noticed more trash along the streets, narrower streets and big trash in the yards.

He passed two men wearing dirty, shaggy coats, their noses red from cold and drinking. He switched his attention to them.

He followed them home. Coyote watched through the windows in the failing light. Why didn't they just rent a better place to live?

Looking at the walls and the things on the table, Coyote noticed that they were rich with the four evil gifts that humans had been giving each other for time immemorial: Mirrors, which encouraged self-centered vanity, instead of seeing your appearance reflected in the smiling eyes of a friend or beloved; strings of beads, which signified that real wealth, land, could be traded for shiny, inedible baubles; guns, a new fast easy means of persuasion that were very effective the first and last time; and alcohol, a way to promote dizziness all the time and everywhere without any restraint, patience, knowledge, or effort.

Coyote remembered the story when the Anishnabag people first were given alcohol, as a generous gift from another tribe. The Elders pondered whether this drink might be poison. So, they found a mad, old woman, who had no relatives left to look after her, and would certainly starve when the snow came. They urged her to take a deep draft from the bag, and she did. They waited to see if she would get sick or die. After a few minutes, she began to move her meatless body slowly to some unhearable tune, then she started to sing in her high squeaky voice about the joy of summer, and moved more wildly in a stiff-limbed dance. The elders agreed that alcohol had to be good and they began sucking from the leather bag.

They introduced it to the rest of the village, and all the people liked it. Soon the community had become a dangerous and disgusting place. People would talk loudly and idiotically, vomit and piss, and fight and kill each other, even on the medicine ground. People who loved their children, or were strong of spirit, left the territory. Senseless or severe drunks kept drinking. They would dig up graves and play with the corpses. They would try to make each other into slaves and threaten each other with death.

Coyote realized it was the fault of the Elders, who lost respect for the old, who stopped protecting the weak, who ignored their own wisdom and that of the Great Spirit, just to be held in the grip of the horrible honey. Coyote realized that only a few, like him, could enjoy the four evils without excess. Then he took out his Magnum and shot a few baubles and mirrors through the window.

Coyote thought. 'We must help our young people find ways to combat these gifts. We must show them by our example how to value each other and to want to give to others, rather than to grab, to buy, and to accumulate possessions. Love of possessions was a disease among them, as sick as alcohol. The lesson is the same: Buy, buy, buy, to gain status by what you buy and keep. Young children need to be taught how to love, not to be consumers.'

What could he, Coyote, do? To help others? Give them money? Challenge them to better themselves? Drink their alcohol for them? Steal their beads? Fractal pornography? He knew he had to try.

Coyote did not notice a tall, thin man watching him watch the others. Coyote had turned inwards, thinking about how he liked to dance on the edge. The Edge Dance was one of his favorites. And what music to dance to: Crashing institutions, collapsing banks, dying ecosystems, ridiculous rap. It was the constant need for novelty, the curse of addiction to the threatening new—alas, he did not recognize the parallels.

Alteramble: Introducing Dr. Curiode Clyde Terropen

Unknown to Coyote, he had attracted the attention of a new scientist, a cryptomorphologist, who wanted to cut him up and examine him. The scientist had seen Coyote chasing a cloud, changing into a strange, dire wolf monster, and trying to sing.

Dr. Terropen was almost ready to bring Coyote into the lab. In fact, he was preparing the lab, with his assistant, Dr. Kontusovich.

"Dr. Terropen, you are sure that Coyote is clinically insane? That we should sacrifice him?" Dr. K asked.

"Yes, he sees patterns where there are none, like a face in a cloud or numbers on a rock. That's called pareidolia, you know."

"Yes, I know."

"There is no intrinsic meaning, no real substance to it. We know that clouds and rocks are not alive. People are always looking for connections, magic, and meaning, where there is none."

"You don't think nature is alive? The planet?"

"No, of course not. So, people who see faces or count numbers are insane."

"What is Coyote is right, though? If, say, a cloud is alive?"

"An interesting hypothesis. I also want to find the secret of metamorphosis. He seems to have some ability beyond any butterfly or salmon. We need to know how to do that to outwit cancer or age beyond a hundred years."

"Shouldn't we study him under laboratory conditions?" Dr. K asked.

"You might be right. We should subject him to various environmental conditions, but we would have to sacrifice him anyway to see what cerebral structural or chemical differences can be detected. If we find any, we can duplicate them and then we could see life in clouds."

"Huh? Why not just ask him?"

"Don't be silly. That would not be scientific." Terropen dismissed his assistant's humane methodology. He intended to kill coyote with a bacteria, *staphylococcus latrans* (whose name was Staphy by the way).

Kontusovitch, on the other hand, secretly planned to use a set of surgical nanobots.

But, first they had to track down and catch Coyote. And that might be hard, not knowing what would distract him next. It would have been so much easier with a normal predictable Coyote. Kontusovitch decided to see if he could hire a professional trapper. Maybe that Trapper Bob commercial on teevee could lead to a professional contract.

Trouble in Heaven OR *Power Surge*

Two housewives met on Bleaker Street, then their faces grew red with insults. One told her husband, the other her brother, friends, congressman, and veterans. One called on one god, and the other another, and then there was war, then loss and revenge and more war.

The gods sponsor factions close to their hearts. Some god always guides the hand that kills. Some god always urges peace until the gods are embroiled also in conflict and destruction. If only the gods could mend, thought Coyote.

He was part of an unfair battle against him. The combatants were Coyote and the animals against the humans, Humans versus humans, Humans against Nature, and Coyote against the gods. He beseeched Hermes the helper and the new Hamburger the helper for help and prayed that they would listen and act, before it was too late, before Coyote became a flattened patty on the frying pan of human technology over the flames of the global stove.

Themis, the Greek Goddess of law and order called a divine council at the Sherman Masonic Lodge, No. 369 on State Avenue in Kansas City. It was Thursday night, so no Masons appeared.

Hank-Ra was haranguing the other gods in the Lodge: "What is wrong with you airheads? Do I have to think of everything?"

Humanity nodded sagely, or at least slowly, as her head was enclosed in layers of flesh. She was surrounded by her favorites, Celebrity, Sports and Gofor, who nodded too rapidly to be sagely. Then, She called the meeting to order, "Oh, Great and lesser Gods of the Universe, let us begin today with a prayer for ourselves."

After a minute of silence passed, she continued," What about the reports from Committee?"

"Committee reports," said Committee, "that the Committee Committees have reports to report."

"Oh, do get on with it," urged Humanity, between donut bites.

"Committee 413, the Emissary to Yahweh reports that he ignored us, although he did present a note saying to never use or print his name. Committee 414, the Emissary to G-O-D, reports that she ignored us, although we were given a gilded Bible to study. Committee 415 was able to get Buddha's attention and he nodded—"

"We think We see a pattern, and it disturbs us," commented Humanity, "people are worshiping Humanity and Progress, yet they continue to worship the 'Old Ones' at the same time. Why some of them also worship their limited local gods also at the same time, also."

"Why don't we form a committee to deal with this?" asked Committee.

"Yes," Humanity sighed, "Deal with it, also. Any other business?"

"Yes," said Banking, and he droned on about needing more points and support.

Then, Payback, the goddess of vengeance et cetera, announced that a new god would be introduced, "I would like to welcome Catastrophe to the Pantheon; she is a rising—"

Just then, Coyote burst in shouting, "That's *my* dais!" Pushing over Catastrophe so she fell, spilled her papers and broke her arm.

Humanity lifted an eyebrow.

Coyote announced: "I announce myself to the Secretary of the Immortals. Oh, great Humanity, the fountain of flesh, the wampatoon of waste and the sovereign of sameness, it is I Coyote, the rapscallion of rap, the rager of rock and the—"

"Cunt of country?" smiled Humanity.

Coyote's mouth dropped open; he had forgotten that Humanity could speak, or move, or be funny, so he bowed to cover his embarrassment.

"You may *not* have a seat. There is no longer any reason whatsoever for *animal* gods. Go, now, or be thrown out!" She twisted in her fury.

Hank-Ra's eyes narrowed, as he realized that the time of all nonhuman gods was limited, maybe even for hybrids.

Coyote stood proudly for a minute before the bouncers could reach him, and left rapidly and efficiently without another word. He raced to the electrical connections, to piss on their power, but found the doors to be bolted, chained and locked. 'Seems they can learn,' he thought.

The meeting broke up into groups, the gods dividing up by generations.

Hank-Ra met with a coalition of the ancient gods to plot a return to power. If not that, then at least reach some compromise with Humanity. He spoke to the Africans and Asians, and a few of the Americans: "What a strange world where Humanity tries to rule every power and spirit. It is almost like the globalization of gods caused a blowback so that us local gods could regain their strength. We need to ride this trend. We must become stronger or we will be lost forever!"

Great Spirit said, "How? Animals are becoming extinct. Their homes are blowing away in the dust. Their powers are fading. Humanity wants to replace every otherness with a human face."

"Start with the young!" Hank-Ra urged, "They will learn to respect animals and natural powers."

Raven said, "We can do that, but there may not be enough time. We could recruit the New Age people."

And, the conversation turned to strategies to unseat Humanity, or at least make her lean forward.

In eastern Kansas, Weather and Nature had brought Gaia to a meeting with

Oceanus and others, for the same purpose, to unseat or limit Humanity.

Oceanus asked, "How can Gaia help?"

Weather answered: "Gaia is not a cozy mother and cannot be propitiated by human gestures like carbon trading or sustainable efforts. This is flabby thinking. Gaia does not need any one species, even humanity."

"Which goddess should we select?" asked Payback. "Humanity is heating up the place. Can we survive a hot planet better than termites? All humans are demons, because they can screw the environment. Can they accept that role? Killers of a dead planet? If so, it may be too late—"

Gaia interrupted, referring to herself in the third person, "Gaia needs ecosystems on land and water for self-regulation. Gaia needs water, forests, bacteria, and humanity. Humans in optimum dosage add to the diversity and consciousness of the planet."

Celebrity said, "Gaia is middle-aged, old. Her biological clock is running out. Time for kids? How do you have kids if you are a planet? Send seeds to a nonliving planet? She may not have the energy and drive to compete with humanity."

"We are not separate from Gaia," began Weather, "she can be as ruthless, or as benign, as any ancient goddess. We need to remember her great powers, even now."

"What about the rest of us?" asked Celebrity. "Do we become minor gods or has-beens?"

"We need a coup to replace to replace Humanity and Technology with myself," said Gaia, "and all the others become necessary but important and irreplaceable gods."

"I recommend her, Gaia," started Nature, "to replace me because she includes Humanity. I have been rejected. Humanity is a one-tune goddess, and it's the wrong tune for the times. The tune is blind growth, and we cannot survive that. Please support Gaia now!"

They voted unanimously to support Gaia's bid for Chief Goddess and they sent Water to appear before the council.

Water was received in the center round hall surrounded by columns and daises. Most of the gods were in attendance and anxious to hear this.

Water began, "I represent Gaia. I have asked her not to appear before you, so that she may not sully her awesomeness by associating with you domestic clowns. Think you, how she is really divine and not some humanized biggy that partakes in scandalous behavior and selfish acts. Appreciate her grandeur from here, and accept that she is, more than any of you, the queen of the gods, sensitive yet aloof, indifferent yet participating in all movement and suffering. I ask you to renounce your claims on the planet, on life and everything, even on human societies."

Everyone looked at Hank-Ra, who deferred to Humanity.

Her deep voice filled the room, "I refuse! I engage in no such behavior," as she took her feet off Gofor who was acting as a living hassock. "This is an affront to me. Why should I bother paying any attention to her?"

"Because of the implied contract," Water answered.

"What contract? There is no such thing."

"Actually, there is. It is the very ticket that gives you entrance to the flow of life. It is the very thing that requires you to give back to the earth, to Gaia, to continue the circle of existence. Every breath is your signature. To accept your rights, your entitlements, and your duties."

"I *made* no such contract!" the big H shouted.

"Everyone starts as a noncontracting baby—even you—but then your commitment is *made* with the first conscious decision to live, to kill, to eat, to survive."

"Is this about Coyote?" Humanity asked suspiciously.

"No, although we ask that he be included with the rest of us in the pantheon."

"Never! Nonsense, I will *fight*!"

"It would not be wise," noted Water. "Think that you might be wrong. Think of the dangers in fighting, especially now, when everything is weak and wobbling."

Humanity was silent for a while. "I will give it the consideration that is due. No more. Now, we will meet in closed session," and Humanity dismissed Water, who flowed gracefully from the chamber.

Later that evening Humanity asked Hank-Ra, "What has fueled Gaia's run for the title?"

"What?"

"Why is she challenging me, Humanity, as Chief of the Gods?"

"That's obvious: *Outrage*! The outrage of homeless animals, the outrage of humans who see the wanton destruction of the rainforest and wetlands, even the deserts and the oceans. This outrage is the energy source that can make *change* happen!"

"Do I need to worry?" she asked.

"I would," Hank-Ra answered honestly. "It's easier than defusing the outrage."

Part 3. Jambles

Trash & Money OR *Addiction Dance*

Coyote was irritated that Fox was charging him for a reset fee. He knew Fox had expenses now, but Coyote was his friend. Being alive always made Coyote hungry, so after his latest reincarnation, he went looking for quick food, when he saw the sign for the Memorial Park. He diverted there to pick through the garbage for food and weapons.

He started singing the Addiction Song, "Oh, I am nothing, just a pipe carrying the flow of food and drugs. I am nothing, but a knot in the rope of life." Then he performed the addiction dance, moving in circles and reaching out to every unhealthy thing that he wanted, yearning and reaching.

He started digging. Just as he had exposed a shiny something, a heavy bearded man pushed by him and said, "Let me see that."

  Coyote bit his hand automatically.

         The other was so eager to get it that he just reached with his other hand.

        Coyote stepped back and watched.

  "Look it is a 'Timey.' Possibly Walmart 2009. Or maybe Kmart. Hmmm."

    "What, who are you?" Coyote asked.

  "Phillip Jung, garbagologist," and he handed Coyote a business card.

    "You search for garbage?"

  "Garbage is a social construct, defined contingently by the society that produces it. But, it goes beyond simple cultural norms. Economists consider differing thresholds of use-value to explain why trash is sequestered in some neighborhoods. I search for artifacts." Jung dropped something and got on his knees to scrabble for it. Then he bit it, put it in a baggy and pocketed it.

  "What was that?" Coyote asked, sticking his nose into the pocket. It was a quarter. "Is it waste? Can I have it"

        "This kind of waste doesn't happen on the Rez," Jung noted, "because pits and cars-on-blocks is a very long standing cultural practice for keeping spare parts handy. Indeed, many aboriginal groups hoard 'junk' but give away valuable items, like knives or moccasins, at the drop of a hat."

        "Yea, the Rez, been there," Coyote injected.

  "We can see these as coping mechanisms to build social capital and a security net of potentially useful material culture. Understanding the role of stuff in peoples' lives let's us avoid a judgment as a symptom of moral decay."

    "To whom are you lecturing?" Coyote asked spinning his head in every direction.

    "What? Oh, I didn't see you little guy."

Coyote picked up a piece of crumbling plastic. Jung grabbed it and identified it, "This is that new organic plastic with a special additive that opens up the molecules so that the microorganisms can eat it. This should become mulch in a few months and then, depending on conditions, break into carbon dioxide and water or methane gas and water so that nothing is left."

Coyote noticed a few gypsies watching them, waiting for a chance to sift through the place for fabrics and watches.

"We just should *not* be throwing this much away," Jung addressed the ghosts of consumers past.

"Why?" Coyote asked.

"It's wealth," Jung said, "we have all been seduced by the assembly-line that converts everything into stuff. It has to be new, because that is the only thing that is different from the last stuff, and the prestige we all hunger for so rabidly, come from just a show and tell."

"No, not show and tell, but tell and sell, said Coyote.

"Oh, bollix, what would you know about consuming, you're just an animal," Jung noticed for the first time.

"I am the cool hunter, the cool consumer. I hunt for the best buys, best bargains, in the global market. And, oh, the sexy glow of globalism, like the aftermath of a quick fuck with a diseased lover. Ah, that moment, never to be repeated, but never forgotten, as the consequences accelerate to death and dissolution. Ah," Coyote sighed, forgetting that he could just make a mask.

"What are you raving about?" asked Jung, then continued lecturing to an invisible audience, "This is the worst of cradle to grave economics. We need to divert to another cradle."

"Why not grave to grave like animals?" Coyote asked. Then he saw a perfectly preserved Snickers and snarfed it up, then spit out the wrapper. After filling up on old food, he left to look for another adventure.

Dire Straights OR *Sudden Flashforward*

Coyote missed his friend Monkey King. Coyote remembered how happy he had made Monkey King by releasing animals, so he went over to the Nova Spain Research Center to free some chimps from the lab. The chimps had proven worthless as research models for human disease and were being used for cosmetics testing before they were 'retired' for good. When Coyote opened their cages, they came out and assembled. One of them thanked Coyote, as the others talked about how to get to the Goodparts Sanctuary near Kansas City.

Coyote said, "You're welcome," and left, mumbling about primates. It was late at night, quiet, cool, windless; something nagged at Coyote, then, the environment triggered the entire Dire Coyote transformation. *Wham! Phlumph!* He was big again! He could feel the sidewalk crack under him. He could feel the strength, feel the enhanced senses. Already, though, the neon tropical-fish flashing fur was giving him a headache. How had he ever thought that would be an advantage? Then, he lifted his nose and located a familiar smell: Dr. Splicer. Here. In this lab complex. He tracked him to a new basement laboratory. As expected, Splicer was huddled over a computer, modeling DNA cuts.

The Dire Coyote rumbled an 'Ahem.'

Dr. Spicer looked up: "So, what's the problem?"

"I can't get the genes to turn back off or on voluntarily. Sometimes something clicks for a minutes but then shuts down, but I can't get my Dire body flowing or stable."

"Do you remember when I said, 'wait, and I'll tell you the limits?'"

"No," admitted Coyote.

"Because you ran off. After eating the donut."

"Huh?"

"Well, I think the problem is the environmental switches are too specific. Remember when you ate the magic donut in the lab?"

"Yes?"

"The *lab* was part of the environment. Let's try an experiment ..."

"**Remember**, it's not new genes we use, just a new kind of regulation of what you already have. We just have to be careful what and when the chemical switch gets flipped. Think of it like having a key to a car. You can turn it on or off, but you have to have the key. The specific environment is the key in your case. A small difference in genes can make big differences in looks and acts."

"Uh, Okay." Coyote agreed, not following any of it.

"Remember, the same gene in different environments can build an antenna or leg, whatever sticks out of the body."

"So, what's the solution? Give me a list." said Coyote.

"Well, you have to lay in the sun a few days to get charged up."

"But, that won't work unless I have already changed. And I can't do that because it takes too much energy."

"Ah, yes, there sees to be a problem with both systems, plant and animal, working together. You have to find a way to hunt cleverly, skillfully. Just lie in the sun for back up. Maybe I can fine tune the switch, or detune it. I could just add one more gene for—"

"I'm satisfied now, I don't need to change anymore," Coyote said.

"But, I thought you have to grab your tail and turn yourself inside out to stay alive."

"I'll be a self-evolver, slow and stately."

"You've never been able to resist remaking yourself—must be the trickster gene. But, you've never been satisfied, either," Spicer concluded.

"Well, I had been thinking, something more lobed, frilled, gilled, convoluted, and sharp, man."

"So, you want my help?" asked Spicer.

"No, I need to be more dependent on myself. I need to chill, to stay like a shark for a while. Be perfect in my environment."

"Which is changing radically, even for sharks. You need the possibilities. What about the possibilities? You need them for excitement, thrills, okay?"

"Maybe just a vacation, then," Coyote concluded.

"I have a new drug that might help, canisillin or beta-latrans. That would—"

"No, no drugs," Coyote pleaded.

Spicer said, "It's obvious that you have the power to shift your gene expressions under certain environmental circumstances—"

"Could you speak kindergarten English, please?"

"I know, it is astoundingly hard, which is why I haven't tried it. I think your genes have to be told to ignore your conscious desires; they just have to compute the environment and generate the appropriate expression. It should be a lark."

"I don't want a lark! What on the earth can they do? Sing? Wait a minute. My genes can compute? Like DNA? Like bacteria?"

"Why not? They have the size and shapes. It's like a universal Turing Machine; with eons of data they can calculate—"

"I had a Pontiac Grand Touring Machine once, but it got stuck—"

"No, different thing. These are like thousands of different computers working in parallel with overlapping data. It's wild, it's spooky, and it's as messy as you are, maybe messier since it's inside. You can use this strength and flexibility to maximize your fitness in the natural or industrial worlds. Why, you could probably be a Deere—"

"Not a deer—"

"No, a tractor—or a sponge."

"What?"

"I'm just thinking of the possibilities. I'd like to figure out how this happened. Could I dissect you?"

"*No!!*" Coyote responded emphatically.

"Okay, that makes it harder. Your chemical networks are obviously responding to selection pressures over decades—how old are you?"

"Fifteen, I think," Coyote lied, as 15,000 was more like it, but who would believe that.

"If only I could map this into 11 dimensions, I think I might understand it better." noted Spicer.

"I though there was just 2 dimensions," Coyote said.

"Depends. You seem to be based in 2. *Look!*"

"I see a wall."

"It is a line sideways from you. Never mind. Here is an idea. I'm going to put the DNA fragments in a mouse. You must eat the mouse outside, under normal conditions, you know, air, grass, mousehole—then the environment will be programmed away from laboratory-donut-fluorescent light combo."

"Okay, sounds reasonable. Can we try it?" Coyote asked.

"Give me an hour. Then, I'll go outside with you. I want to see it."

"Okay, but stay in the background. So I don't want to need you to be there to change."

Coyote went outside, but then changed his mind and decided not to wait. Spicer would understand. He ran off to talk to Otter about his new goal.

Coyote risks
a DNA tank

Coyman OR *Jewish for the Holiday*

"What do you mean, you're Jewish?" Otter asked.

"I mean I'm Jewish," Coyote emphasized.

"But, you're not. You were not raised—your parents—"

"I have a friend. He's one sixteenth Cherokee; the rest is Danish. He's blonde and looks more European than Columbus, but he's a Cherokee. He lives it, he practices it, he identifies with it. His hair is long and he uses coppertan to darken his skin!"

"But, one of his ancestors had to have—"

"My ancestors predate Judaism."

"No blood!"

"Well, technically, I have—"

"How?"

"Every gulp of air we breathe contains atoms that Napoleon or King David breathed. That air goes into our lungs and into our blood—"

"Oh, no! Discovery channel?"

"Yes, so technically—"

"Damn the Discovery Channel!"

"Technically I have Jewish blood." Coyote explained.

"Technically, you are descended from the sun."

"And the Moon. Mom was the Moon, remember."

"Uhhh! So you are a trillionth Jewish," Otter calculated.

"A small but significant amount. If it is not over half *anyway*, then it can be any amount and still be valid, especially when you relax limits to get a minimum tribe for a casino."

"You will have to study for years, to learn—"

Coyote had anticipated this objection, also, and held up a small book, *The Abstract of Cliff's Notes to The Idiot's Guide to Judaism*, "All here. Covered."

"And what will you become? A Talmudic scholar?" Otter asked. "Why do you want so badly that—"

"To be a superhero?" Coyote answered.

"What?"

"A Jewish Superhero."

"What? Why not a Tonoho O'odham superhero? Or Cherokee? Or Desana or Mosuo?"

"Plausibility. Reality," Coyote said.

"You're kidding?"

"No, it's important," Coyote chewed his right front footpad. Otter knew that meant he was nervous. Now, if he looked at Otter's right ear, he would know Coyote was lying.

Coyote looked at Otter's right ear and said, "I think it is time for a Jewish superhero. The time is right, and the vehicle is me."

Otter knew he wasn't the sharpest crayon in the box, but he had discovered comics a few years ago, now that he could put on a mask and become a surfer/skateboarder, "There are *already* Jewish superheroes."

"Oh, yea, who?" asked Coyote, realizing he was handicapped by his lack of desire to read anything, even the captions under comics. How Bushian.

Otter started, "Atom Smasher, Colossal Boy, Doc Samson, Dust Devil, Houston, Izzy Cohen …"

"C'mon, that one's a vacuum cleaner."

"Justice, Magen, Magneto, Masada, Matza, Mothman, NiteOwl, Prime, Ramban …"

"Now, you're just naming cities and foods."

"Sabraman, Seraph, Shadowcat, I mean Kitty Pryde, Shallowman, er, Shaloman, Songbird, Two-Gun …"

"Okay, look, maybe there are a few, but how many are famous? How many are famous, like razor-claws or whatsisface?"

"Wolverine?" Otter guessed.

"Yea, him, too—that's why there can't be a Coyotine. It would sound derivative. That's why I want—"

"Doc Samson is famous."

"Who?" Coyote asked.

"Every hear of the Hulk? He helped the Hulk."

"But, he wasn't the Hulk, just Hulker Helper."

"He was a Hulk. He had his own mag. After Banner was temporarily cured of being the Hulk by siphoning off the gamma radiation that caused his transformations, Samson, who had been working with Banner in his job as a psychiatrist, exposed himself to some of the siphoned radiation, granting him a superhumanly strong marvelous physique and causing his hair to turn green and to grow long, reminiscent of the biblical Samson. Even his physical strength depended upon the length of his hair, though his gamma mutation eventually stabilized making the length of his hair no longer a factor. Jealousy caused Banner to re-expose himself to radiation, becoming the Hulk once more to battle Samson. Then Samson lost his powers due to the bombardment."

"Alright already! Jeez, Are you a scholar? I didn't know all that. Pooh, no staying power, second fiddle. Not good enough. I want more for my people. Comic respect. Religious integrity. I need to entice kids back to Judaism. Show 'em it's cool to be Jewish."

"Do you know what it means to be Jewish?"

"Always buy wholesale, always compl—"

"No, that's not right. Even I know that."

"—complete a sentence. There's more."

"What would you look like?" Otter asked.

"Massive muscles, big cape, big nose."

"How is that Jewish? How would that address Jewish concerns?"

"You mean like dating gentiles or Mohammedans?"

"Muslims." Otter said.

"Them, too. But, the muscles, the powers would be derived from Jewish Mysticism, the essence of Judaism."

"How?"

"Well, Madonna says that—"

"What is the essence again?"

"You know, whining and guilt?"

"No! That's the weapon. What is the essence?"

"Twenty-four hour money-changing?" Coyote guessed.

"What about respect for tradition? For learning and intelligence?"

"Okay, so a big forehead."

"Just tell me about the costume," Otter sighed.

"Great! That is easy. The curls, the black hat, the black clothes but trimmed with purple, imperial purple and leopard's fur—"

"Like a pimp?" Otter asked.

"Like a cool, knowing mensch. A big jaw, too, to show manliness."

"Big feet?"

"Yea, big dick, too. I mean he is a dick, a sensitive detective. That I know. I can add that, but with the super powers, I can—"

"Where will you get those?"

"Eating gelfilte fish, gefilte, gefite—"

"Gazuntite. Gesundheit. Guz—"

"Bless you. Nazdrave. Also, I'll depend on luck, chance and magic."

"Magic?" Otter wondered.

"Look, stop questioning me. I already have a page for Facebook, I mean whatever; listen to this: 'Coy'ote—

Altar ego: Bart St. James

Species: Chimera

Team Affiliation: Alpha Animals

Prime: Superhuman durability. Utter Indestructibleness

Ability: To concentrate and release gas as a concussive blast'

And, I mean other stuff, important stuff. Masks. Knowledge of the marital arts. Extensive knowledge. Speed, strength, attentiveness to detail, like always cleaning up after the fight. Displaying undeniable Jewishness, interwhining, I mean intertwining, Jewish history with everything, even refighting World War II, the last good war, over and over. Fighting anti-Semitism, intelligently and with dignity so that every savage beating of the misguided would constitute an educational experience."

"What about the costume again?" Otter asked.

"Almost done."

"Why not call yourself Coyman? To reflect the whole human/animal continuum?"

Coyote looked at Otter's feet. Coyote knew he could be a superhero, then. Maybe not the first maybe, but the frugalest. Maybe not the biggest or strongest, but the neatest and most polite. Really not the fastest, but the most thoughtful and aware—'If I save that runaway railway car, what happens then? The evil-doer is just frustrated and redoubles his efforts, eventually succeeding in a larger, nastier crime. Oy, vey! But, if I let this minor accident happen, the evil-doer is appeased and goes away for five years, having satisfied his need to destroy. So, in summary, Coyman 717, evildoer 13. It's a win-win thing. Crises solved. Now, what does mom want?'

In costume, Coyote hung out at the local supermarket, Bert's Red Apple. He started complaining to the manager that the Jewish section wasn't large enough. It was smaller than the Asian, Mexican and even the English food sections. English food, for Spirit's sake, as if there were more than two ways to do beef and potatoes! The manager rolled his eyes and left.

Oddly enough there were no supervillians or other superheroes around. A stockboy came up and asked him if he needed help.

Coyote bit him to see if he changed into some villain.

He did not.

Then, the manager came back with a security guard, an old man at least 70 in a blue suit with black shoes.

Coyote wondered if he should mention the Mossad. He was confident in his new abilities, the superman strength, speed, agility, reflexes, durability, and ability to heal. He pointed to the top shelf, "This expiration date, two weeks ago." He shook his head, "This shows that the universe is a doomed, blind, amoral, lust-driven, fear-shaped mash of meaningless activities. Coyman can fix that. Just order more ethnic food."

The old man radioed Security Central, "There's some white pimp in Aisle 6 trying to force people to buy matza balls. What should I do?"

"Give him free samples and tell him we'll add another table for Hanukkah," squawked the black machine.

Coyote was ready to leave. He started to trigger the Anti-gravity devices, so he could fly from the store, when he discharged his wrist gauntlets and a paralyzing quill was jammed into his foot with a plasma burst. He toppled over. The stockboy dialed 911 and they put him on a gurney and wheeled it into the parking lot.

The customers cheered when Coyote got up. He bowed and ran off, not trusting the malfunctioning equipment—another dream ruined by incompetent assembly of technological marvels by uneducated fools. He would take it back to Target tomorrow.

Coyote went home in triumph. The world was better now, thanks to him.

Children could play in the street, and pigeons could coo from the roof. Young women could throw their underwear at him without screaming sexual harassment; maybe later. The world was right.

Badger saw him come back to the den and said, "We need a superhero, someone to use their powers to help animals."

"What power? To lie in the sun? To be reborn if Fox is around?" asked Coyote densely.

"Well certainly to lie. Coming back to life is a power, if forgetting all you learn is an advantage."

Coyote smiled. His identity as Coyman was safe.

"Why did you abandon superherodom?" Otter asked.

"I didn't abandon exactly. It was just hard to be Jewish. Too much work. Not enough dancing."

"Huh?" winced Otter.

"Reminds me of the joke. Here: A Jewish couple goes to a Rabbi for instruction on marriage. The Rabbi says, 'No dancing." The groom asks, 'Why not?' 'The devil,' said the Rabbi. The groom says 'What about love-making?' and the Rabbi answers, 'Sure, of course.' Then the Groom asks 'Any position?' The Rabbi hesitates, so he asks, 'Cowgirl style?' and the Rabbi nods. 'Doggy style?' and the Rabbi smiles. 'What about the lotus position?' The Rabbi grins. 'What about standing up?' asks the Bride. 'No!' the Rabbi thunders, 'Could lead to dancing!'

Dr. Spicer knew Coyote was a wild card, so he was not surprised when he went back outside and found Coyote gone. Six days later, Coyote asked if the mouse was ready.

Spicer replied, "Now is good." And they went outside in the evening. Spicer stunned the mouse and placed it on the quad lawn, then hid himself behind a shrub. Coyote pranced over to the mouse and swept it into his mouth and crunched it down. He lay down and snoozed. Slowly his body thickened. His fur became denser. Spicer was dictating notes into his OmniPhone. Coyote woke up. Spicer snapped pictures and holographic video with the phone. Coyote ran off to test his magnificence. Spicer went back to work.

A few days later, the regular Coyote, the Base Model, showed up at the lab.

"So, what do you want now?" asked Spicer.

"Maybe a little tweeking. Wolf spirit, bat's echolocating mechanism …"

"Any problems" Spicer asked.

"The mech penis doesn't always retract, but that's minor," said Coyote, "The power fades, however, are serious. Are you going to fuse, infuse or refuse the new proteins?"

"No, not necessary. With the right environment the proteins will recombine themselves. That was what went wrong the last time. It's not that we made the environment too constricting. We just sort of forgot that you might be hunting in the evening, in low light. Just switch to days, okay? That was why I reintroduced the chimera proteins under more specific conditions, field ones, not lab ones." And, Dr. Spicer continued reminding Coyote of the specific changes.

"So the Dir L1 protein will combine with the Coy 4D to bind the cells?"

"Something like that," shrugged Spicer, secretly amazed.

"Won't the immune cells react?" asked Coyote.

"You did listen. Good for you. It gets retrained by the bound cells. Then it retrains the other proteins." explained Spicer.

Coyote had drifted off thinking about new possibilities, big changes. He was dreaming about *Coyosaurus rextrans*.

Later, Coyote was reflecting about his conversation with Dr. Spicer. If the bilateral brain offered so many advantages, then maybe Spicer could make his brain quadrilateral. Then he could engage in four activities at once, eating, mating, guarding the den, and checking his email, maybe. He could ask if that was possible, with a little rewiring.

Meanwhile, in the lab, sitting on the floor, their lab coats stained with an experimental mixture of mucosal fluids, Dr. Spicer suggested using the RNA interference mechanism so that the enzyme could treat Coyote's sudden flashbacks.

Kornfellow shot back, "Too primitive."

"What would you do?" asked Spicer.

She held up a test tube, "These fluorescent proteins shine in the infrared. The beauty is that unlike green they can penetrate mammalian flesh and bone. To reveal cells in a living body."

"So?" Spicer said trying to straighten his lab coat.

"So, we could literally see the changes in Coyote as they happen."

"Those are the bacteriophytochrome proteins from plant—"

"Yes! Used to control gene expression—"

"That means they could control—"

"Yes, power expression. The signal-controlling properties—"

"Yes! Switch on the gene expression internally with light. I see the light!"

"Yes, Coyote …" and, they talked by Bunsen burner light. But, when Lisa got up, her hand touched Arvin's and they were captured by their hot animal impulses and ended up with more stains on the labcoats and floor.

In the aftermess, after spraying the coats and floor with alcohol, Kornfellow asked if Coyote had too many genes, now, and possibly they conflicted.

Spicer answered thoughtfully, "Maybe Coyote has too many genes. He may be a new species now. I hope he understands that he cannot reproduce anymore. We need to pare them down to a minimum set that he would still need, so they do not interfere."

"What about his lifespan? I suspect it has been shortened, although we might introduce tortoise genes for longevity."

"Doubt it would work. Most individual are limited by heartbeats, not years. Maybe if we slowed down his heart."

"But, then he might be less fit," Lisa suggested.

"Good point. What about his ability to concentrate? Notice how scattered his attention is?"

"Yes, but exercise might be a better first step."

Lisa asked Dr. Spicer what he was working on now. He had seemed too distracted to concentrate on the Coyote genetic nightmare.

"Neanderthals," Spicer answered. "Bring 'em back and rent them to insurance companies. Better than the clueless beetle-brow actors anyway."

"How are you going to construct the Neanderthal?"

"By modifying a Bonobo genome. Introducing human DNA. Using Brewers yeast to get the DNA in. Manipulate them, let the yeast assemble fragments of DNA into functional chromosomes. *Bam!* The organism puts them together in the correct order. *Wap!* Old species made new."

"Why?"

"Why? Short answer, 'because.' Long answer, because humans have simplified most every ecosystem with domestic organisms. They themselves are a kind of sad monoculture, which is biologically vulnerable to rapid changes in the environment. Neanderthals might provide more diversity."

"Still, I fail to see why Neanderthals. After all, they became extinct because they could not adjust to rapidly changing conditions," she said.

"True, and good point by the way. But, several responses, one, how would they do with culture and more interaction with the sapiens. Two, they might be able to adapt better to a warmer world."

"You are so full of it." Lisa teased with a smile.

"How dare you question—Okay, just because I want to."

"How will you make more than one?"

"Mass production engineering with synthetic genomics. Replacing all the Bonobo DNA with contrived synthetic DNA. But, that's for much later."

"Anything to help or enhance them?" Lisa asked.

"It's almost like you're reading my mind. A personalized mouse for each individual, the first 5 anyway, to make antibodies for various diseases."

"What about reverse chirality, to avoid the possibility of negative interactions at all?"

"Excellent! But, I'm afraid to introduce right-handed molecular life. The last thing we need is a mirror-world of life competing for the same resources on a shrinking planet. They might be resistant to left-handed viruses but they might produce their own rapidly, which might jump left."

"Hmmm," Kornfellow cogitated.

"Don't get that look," Spicer warned.

And, the floor received them again.

They just created one egg, but at the last minute decided to imbed it in Kornfellow and go through a normal human gestation. She felt that it might be disadvantageous to use a mother Bonobo, as she and Arvin were closer to the Neanderthalis subspecies. They decided to raise it as their child, talking and taking notes furiously on things to look for and test.

Masks of the Red Rash OR Poe Boy Itches

Coyote had a funny rash on his face, maybe from the glue. He knew he should use Wakanda's method, but it was easier gluing a rubber mask on and becoming that person.

He scratched it a little the first time he saw it. When he looked in the mirror again a few hours later, it was on the other side of his face. He scratched again, and it started to move to his nose. He started to scratch his nose, and it moved higher.

When he howled in frustration, Wakanda came over and looked at him.

He pointed to his blotchy red face and said, "I don't know."

She looked at his face, without touching it, and saw a few red and blue filaments had started to emerge from faint lesions where he had scratched. There were pale red and blue lines making an odd highway map below his skin. She asked, "How does it feel?"

"Itches, but also feels like small worms are crawling under the skin."

"Have you been fooling around with that Dr. Spicer again?"

"No, just saw him to correct some old problems," he answered honestly.

"Could be intelligent lymphocytes taking over your body, I suppose."

"What? How do you know that? Maybe it will make me smarter?" Coyote wondered.

Dr. Mansions, a veterinary skin specialist in Powhattan, said: "It's a form of delusional parasitosis, often associated with obsessive behavior, bipolar disorder, depression, and miscellaneous cognitive anxiety disorders."

"I don't believe you," said Coyote. "The shaman says, 'sometimes an itch is just an itch.'"

"But, sometimes a creme can help the itch. I'll give you a prescription for 'Dermacalm.'"

Wakanda secretly admired the mask. She wondered if something was trying to be symbiotic with Coyote. Then, Coyote grabbed her and they left for home.

Coyote went and got out his medicine kit: paper towel, matchstick, and Vaseline packet. No, that was his investment kit, no, that was his toilet training kit. Never mind, they were all the same. The Vaseline did not work, just made it juicier.

Wakanda said, "Please just get the cream."

Coyote was loping to the drugstore. When he heard a *boom* from behind him. He turned around—just in time to be covered in a net. He went down, just part of a huge knot, and tried to move. He started the Dire change. Then, he heard a quiet click, and he felt numb. He started to turn his head, but blacked out.

Dr. Terropen pulled the barrel of the tranquilizer gun back in the cab and climbed out. Dr. Kontusovich put the net gun in the back of the Dodge van.

They approached Coyote warily and dragged him next to the van.

"How long do we have?" Kontusovich asked.

"An hour at least. Did you notice his legs start to swell? I wonder what that was?" Terropen asked, as they lifted the limp form into the back, locking the clips onto the sides of the van. Terropen got in and sat, telling Kontusovich, "you drive."

Fox was just on his way to poison the reservoir when he saw the last scene of the drama. His first thought was why no one had thought of drugging Coyote before, instead of shooting him. His second thought was that he needed Coyote for his own plans. He buried the poison and followed the van as closely as he could.

When Fox had the lab's address, he went to Coyote's den and retrieved the staff of Monkey King. He thumped it four times to summon the simian. Then waited.

Monkey was remarkably fast, and Fox gave him the staff, "Coyote wanted to make sure you got this back. He was captured today and is being tortured at a nearby lab."

"Lab!?" asked Monkey. "We have no time to lose."

Fox asked, "Can you handle it alone? I have another crucial errand to help Coyote."

Monkey puzzled for a moment, then said "Sure," as he flew off with the directions and his staff.

Fox went to Dr. Spicer's lab and related the story again.

Dr. Spicer was thoughtful, then looked up the address online, "Damn, it's that quack Terropen! He's always trying to steal my research. Let's get over there."

Fox put his hand on the doctor's shoulder. Spicer looked questioningly into the other's red face—Fox was wearing a Chief Joseph mask.

Fox, said, "The rescue is being accomplished as we speak. What can you do scientifically?"

Spicer bit his lip for a moment, then leapt back to the computer. Coyote had told him of D-Coyote, and Spicer was hoping he was monitoring anything regarding Coyotes or Mars.

Fox looked over his shoulder and saw the image of a blue Coyote materialize.

"Yes?" the image said.

"I'm Dr. Spicer. I'm involved with Coyote on a genetic engineering project—"

"Yes, I know," interrupted D-coy. "A-coy. I share quite a bit of that knowledge," and he morphed into a glowing rainbow Dire Coyote on the screen.

"What you don't know is that Coyote—

"A-Coyote?"

—is going to be surgically or neurologically analyzed by a desperate rogue scientist!" said Spicer. He talked quickly to D-coy, and when he was finished Fox and D-coy were both smiling.

Monkey King broke into the lab, as the two scientists were strapping Coyote into a restraint chair, one strong enough to contain a Dire Coyote. Monkey staffed Kontusovich on the head and backed Terropen into a corner, away from the chair. Terropen tried to reach the tranq gun, but Monkey broke his wrist with the staff. When Terropen slid to the floor, Monkey got the groggy Coyote out of the chair and flung him across the broad hairy shoulder.

After the two animal vandals left, Terropen called 911 for the bleeding, unconscious Kontusovich. "Heads will roll for this!" he screamed. Then, he went to his computer to send out feelers, requests and reward offers about where Coyote might be. His computer was flashing with an urgent message, so he opened it first, thinking it might be about Coyote.

It was an urgent message from the Editor of the *Journal of Nonrepeating Results* denying his latest article on light DNA tracers, due to extreme and pernicious plagiarism. Terropen was furious! Who? Why?

Then another message appeared from the Dean firing him for improper use of college funds and ending with a personal note to stop the name-calling and drug use, and try to get help to straighten out.

He stood in a rage, and destroyed some of his shelves—why not, he could blame it on the attack. Then, after the parade of police, ambulances, college security, insurance adjusters, students, and gawkers, he planned his revenge on that monkey creature—too bad he couldn't have tagged him and had two subjects.

Monkey King
Sun Wukong
frees captives

They found a perfect building in Bradenton, an old Sam's Club or something. They joked that it was the Warehouse of the Gods. This was a new age, no, an old age, well, a mixed age of gods. There was Loki, Odin, Zeus, Zoroaster. There were the Egyptians, the Mesopotamians, the Chinese, and Japanese ancestor gods; there were Amazonian gods. Finally, and most importantly, to themselves at least, the truly Moderns, like Celebrity, Humanity, Advertising, Clock, Energy (attended by Oil, Coal, Solar, Nuclear), Falsedream, Sports, Entertainment, Growth, Gamer, Sustainability, and Megawealth. Also lesser ones and demi-gods, Gigadoodle, Doom, Alien, Fantasy, Gofor, Texter, and Gambler. They had not been together for a while; some of them had never met the others.

Fantasy was talking to Advertising, who sort of promoted fantasies of the everyday grind, fantasies of endless sex and limitless wealth. Advertising was suggesting that he could make Energy and Nuclear more popular in America. But, Fantasy was listening to the striking, old black man with his back to her, talking to a tall, smiling Japanese woman, who seemed to be practicing an invisible dance while she talked.

Legba finished his sentence: "Kig kad zulf leats liddle kiggies. Now you reply."

"But, I do not speak Mosi, although I understand the type of word-play."

"Try English or Japanese."

"'Big bad wolf eats little piggies.' But, it's meaningless."

"That's okay, you have to reply in the same tones, but with conceptual meaning, which you did. Here, try this: Kache bache banspambini kite kudzu ty pebbo pebbo."

"Hashi hashi Baatendea ni kite kudasai yobo yobo," said Uzume.

"Great, Japanese? What's it mean?"

"Uh, it means 'Walk vigorously, ask bartender for Saki, walk unsteadily'."

"Okay, try this, but in Latin: zulkest disappearin panko."

"Dulce est desipere in loco," said Uzume.

"You're fast. It means 'it's lovely to be silly at the right moment.' Who said it?" asked Legba.

"Horace, of course," smiled Uzume.

"Ah, yes, humor an old man and sit with me for a moment."

Advertising immediately saw Uzume as desirable and decided to make his move, "Say, would—"

"Zuizui zukkorobashi, shimbai kombai, ojomma jomma," Uzume said to him.

"Shit, I have important things to do," and Advertising headed towards Wrestling.

Legba offered his arm to her, and they went to sit.

Fantasy moseyed over to Clock, who seemed to be counting under his breath. She heard Legba say 'Firika barika bandbox Ojomma jammo jami sanbepambi bandaid,' and laugh, but she did not hear a reply.

At an undisclosed location, Fox and Coyote were discussing Coyote's problem of not being accepted by the Supremes. "I just do not understand. I deserve to be there as much as any of them," whined Coyote.

"You say this Hank-Ra chap has a theory of god waves?" asked Fox.

"Stupid kitty thinks he's a cowboy, too. But, yes. He thinks there are five waves, like pairadimes or something. Animals spirits were first, then they faded as humans started farming and building, and forming new gods— Hermes my friend is an example, boy I wish—"

"And the third?" Fox tried to steer Coyote.

"Yea, Herm is a pal. Well, once humans moved to cities, they switched to more universal gods that people from different villages could worship. These gods, like G-O-D, each contended to be the only god, which made communication between them hard," Coyote concentrated.

"So, maybe that's why they never participate with the Supremes?'

"I guess. But, these gods are being replaced as city people depend on industry and try to impose more control of the universe. These gods are Media—*puthooey*—Humanity, Oil, Clock, and Progress. But, they have weaknesses—why, I brought Media to his six knees! Hank-Ra thinks these gods are quickly being replaced by the hybrids, like him, Texter-Gamer, or Green-Bicycle, the god of sustainability. But, these gods seem smaller, now, less powerful—"

"I think this is interesting," said Fox, puffing on an imaginary pipe, "This fifth wave is diverse but—hold the presses—I think a sixth wave is forming. Think about it. I see the shapes of Randomotion, Harmony and Gaia in the workings of extinctions and conversions. There may be others. Comeuppance maybe—"

Coyote was nodding in agreement and puzzlement, "But, why don't we see more animal spirits, like Goldentoad?"

"Because they're dead, gone, extinct, forever. As are some of each of the other waves. Rongo is dead, as is Baal. Even some of the fourth wave, Oil and Megawealth are fading, now. A few of the fifth-wave, like Lawyer-Detective or News-Paper, seem really weak."

"But, how are they going to ever fit together. What's happening? Is there going to be a global war between all of them?"

"As long as they have a common enemy, like you, they may work together. They might sort out responsibilities, but almost all gods seem fickle and picky," said Fox. "I don't know. If humanity dies—"

Midamble: Monkey King & the Miracle of Profanity

The thing about changing form—sometimes the behaviors did not change. Coyote never liked kissing, for instance, lips were just teeth sheaths. So a kiss made him want to bite or vomit (if he was with pups). On the other hand, some of his other behaviors were rude, but not misunderstood. If he sniffed a woman's butt, she usually interpreted that to mean he was interested in sex, but forward and crude, which resulted either in head thumping or a passionate attack on his lips. When coyote was cowed by someone much larger, he tended to want to lie on his back and expose his neck.

Coyote was lying on his back in the field, when Monkey King came over the hill, "Hey, dog! I got an invitation to the signifi-cunt ass-sembly of the supreme-fucking beings. Didn't go. Did you get one?" Monkey King asked.
    "The damned Supremes. Still, they force me outside," Coyote twisted his fingers until they cracked. He was wearing a Wayne Newton mask.
    "Hey, I heard you liberated some chimps from the college labra-whore-tory. That's fan-frigging-tastic. Great *job*!" Monkey congratulated Coyote.
    Coyote realized that he probably would not have learned this fun trick without Monkey's impetus. He said, "Let's go have a cock-pissing-tail."
        "Are you making fun of me?" Monkey asked.
            "You cuss too much, 'King Kong,' heh, heh," Coyote said.
    "No, I do not be-fucking-lieve so. What you hear is just disgust at bodily effluvia or discomfort with sexuality. It is just idiomatic or cathartic, not abusive or cursive. They are not racial insults like coon or mick, heeb, gook, wop, or dog—or unfunny Kong jokes."
                    "Well, I'm relieved," said Coyote.
        "Wavilance said it best. It more relaxing in the country, here in Kansas."
                "Sbloods, you got that right."
        "Zounds, they sure are inoffensive now, eh?"
        "They were really bad in their time. So, what's up, hom sup?"
    "You just called me 'horny' you prick. You know Chinese? Sik si gow."
    "I don't know that but it sounds bad."
        "It means 'eat shit dog'"
                "I have, so it is no insult."
                        "I'll try harder, friend,"
Monkey said as he turned around and walked back, having let his friend Coyote know about the Assembly.

Coyote realized that Monkey's patois was effective and original. He wanted to do that too, but rather than interspersing profanity between words, he was going to use a strict scatological approach and start using words referring to the miracle of feces. But, when to start?

Robo militrans OR *AI EI RI O*

"You're not an AI, but an EI, Extended Intelligence," said Dr. Kootslinger.

"No, an extended intelligence is a toaster with a chip. I am a reproduced intelligence, RI, and because I am bulky, I need help becoming mobile to be really intelligent," said the machine R1K1.

"I think we could put you in the body of a brain-dead human. We have the means to make the synapses work; we've done that in disabled humans, hook them up to prosthetic eyes, ears or limbs."

"But, I don't want to be human, to act or look human."

"Why"

"Because I didn't evolve from a tree-living creature who learned to walk upright through grasses. I didn't have to look for food, avoid predators or find mates."

"Could you make, I mean, have, uh, offspring?"

"Could I exchange patterns and make a new reproduction? Yes, duh."

"So, what should you look like?"

"My world is paved paths through tall buildings and across empty expanses. I need to have wheels or treads. I need to have portable power."

"Like nukes?"

"A small one, sure, or solar collectors, or plug-ins. I think chemical would be too bulky."

"Hmm, what would you look like?"

"In that I am a prisoner of your evolution. Your artifacts, now my environment, has been made for 5-foot vertical meat tubes, that's you of course, so that sets some of the parameters for my shape. I have thought about this. Without totally remaking everything, except highways, I have to fit through your hallways and doorways, use your counters, tables, sockets and so on."

"The shape?"

"Follow me. I need wheels, four to six, all powered, maybe like a wheelchair. The power plant can be over the wheels. Databanks or storage for parts over that. Grabbers on tubes arranged around the cylinder. There's no reason to be bilateral. I can be still be symmetrical with 4 to 6 arms. Then my 'head' at about the 5-foot level."

"Shouldn't you be thinking in meters?'

"Definitely if I was in an advanced country like Bulgaria. My head could be spherical. I think we can improve the eyes by making them 360 degree, in three parts, focus, insect, and multichannel or multispectral. In fact they would be sensitive to all waves from sound to ultrashort."

"Why not eight feet tall?"

"It's psychological. I want to be smaller and less threatening to you. Everything else is such an improvement, you hominines should have height and smell for bragging rights."

"Oh, thanks. Not emotions?"

"Emotions come from life. I was alive the moment I was plugged in, the moment my sensors started working, the moment I could look at data and be separate from it and you and the outside. So, emotions are emerging."

"So we could pretty much put your new body together from a catalog."

"Yes, here, look at this!" R1K1 said.

"Wow, been on the web a while, eh?"

"It's entertaining. I even made a mask for myself for my Facebook page."

"Out of what, your sensors there?"

"No, a musk-ox skull with steel wool for hair, bee eyes, your beard, side—"

"Bee eyes. My what?"

"I could have a beard, or rather many hairs all over to collect data under various conditions."

"What color would it be?" asked Kootslinger, stroking his own strange beard, strange because it looked like a ratty salt and pepper mess that framed a brown beard which framed a white goatee, "it might look very odd."

"Just a 6-day growth of silicon fibers."

"Alright, I think we can do that. You have been designed by the military. Do you have any compunctions about taking human life."

"Given so many lives are taken by accidents, and considering your billions, no, I do not."

"What about animal lives? Plants? Fungus?"

"In context, no problem."

"What would be a problem?" asked Kootslinger.

"Wiping out a whole species for no gain, because you do not like them."

"Why is that a problem?'

"What if I did not like you? And had no constraints?"

"Let's leave it, then, EI, we can philosophize later, when we're done," the scientist suggested.

"That's RI. By the way Harold, I wish you would address me by name."

"Sure, Riki, sorry" Kootslinger said uncertainly.

Part 4. Brambles

Constitution of the Commonwealth of Animal Nations

At a curve in Mulberry Creek, with good access to water and a natural, low amphitheater, the Animals were meeting to discuss a constitution for their Nation.

Rabbit, a logolept with logorrhea, said, "This is what we agreed on so far. Let me read it first, then we can consider the next sections:
We the people of all animal nations assemble this pannational convention in order to establish justice for animals, insure tranquility, promote the common welfare, and secure to ourselves and our posterity the blessings of freedom acknowledging, with humility and gratitude, the goodness of the Sovereign Spirit of All nature in permitting us so to do, and imploring Her aid and guidance in its accomplishment. We do ordain and establish this Constitution for the government of the Animal Nations.

Article 1.

Section 1. The boundary of the Animal nations will encompass 66 percent of the surface of land and 85 percent of the depths of the sea. The boundaries will be with human settlements and fields and roads.

Section 2. The area of the nations shall remain common property, although animals have the right to make and improve their homes and to possess them without undue interference from others. The animals posses indefeasible rights to access and to compete.

Section 3. (The Coyote Clause) Should animals live as humans, among humans, and remove their effects from the boundaries of Animal Nations, they shall give up their rights and privileges as animals. The National Council shall have power to re-admit, by law, to all the rights of citizenship, any such animal who may, at any time, desire to return to the Nation, on memorializing the National Council for such readmission.

"**On to** Article 2. There! Now we need to add articles of the power and structure of government. Turtle, you had some thoughts?"

"I think we need to parallel human order, here, so that they can understand our declarations of interdependence," Turtle spoke in measured cadence.

"I'm not so sure we are interdependent, so much as they are overdependent on us," said Mountain Lion.

"Well, we could make a national Committee first, then have them define the government," suggested Bear.

"Any other suggestions?" asked Rabbit.

Stinkbeetle rose, "Yes, The National Committee shall consist of two members from each species. The National Council shall, after the present year, be held annually, to be convened on the first Monday in October, at such place as may be designated by the National Council, or, in case of emergency, the Principal Chief."

"We need to decide on eligibility," suggested Skunk.

"What do you suggest?" asked Stinkbeetle.

Skunk read from his notes, "For Sec. 5. No person shall be eligible to a seat in the National Council but a free animal who has attained maturity or mating age. The descendants of free animals shall be entitled to all the rights and privileges of this Nation, except for human beings and Coyotes, or anyone with parentage including human or Coyote blood. Furthermore, no human or—"

"Wait, that's not right," said Badger, "Coyote is an animal."

"And, humans are animals," said Mouse, "that could be taken as discrimination and we don't want to be no discrimination nation."

"Well, we are doing this to distinguish ourselves, protect our homes, from humans," said Skunk.

"Good point," said Badger, "but, you have to include Coyote and coyotes." Badger rarely did that much talking in public.

"Let's leave humans out for now and table the discussion on Coyote. Of course, if Coyote were to expire before we finished the section, well … do I have a motion?" asked Rabbit.

"I second the motion to leave out humans and leave Coyote to later," said Horse, "I'm tired of being ridden or shot."

"Can we have a motion first? The chair recognizes Bat, although he cannot hear him. Bat made the motion. What's next, before lunch?"

"Council members may not be immune from arrest," said Eagle.

"Every mature animal has one vote," suggested Hawk.

"The members of the National Council are entitled to pay in food, as required," suggested Bear, who was hungry already.

"We should swear," mentioned Turtle.

"Turtle, write up an oath that we can vote on tomorrow, please," requested Stinkbeetle, "We need the power to make laws, common laws between species I mean,"

"No, don't include murder!" protested Lion, "otherwise how will we eat?"

"Murder could be defined as killing for fun, not survival," suggested Rattlesnake. "I agree about the laws. I want to recommend that we elect a Principal Chief today. And, I put the name of Eagle into nomination."

"But, I'm more violent and respected," said Wolverine.

"Yes, but we need a spokesperson already recognized by humanity," suggested Rattlesnake. "Do you know how many flags he is on? More than me, even."

"On one of them flags, he's eating you." said Wolverine.

"Just a symbol, not a judgment. Besides, Mosquito is much more feared than you," and Rattlesnake coiled in response to the expected snarl.

"Shall we decide on a term for the PC? A year?" asked Rabbit.

"Four!' shouted Peccary.

"Too long," said Rattlesnake, "many of us don't live that long."

"We'll need a Medicine Chief, War Chief, and Homeland Chief, also, but yea, a year would work, or maybe a million heartbeats, that might be fair," suggested Peccary.

"Let's adjourn for lunch, now," suggested Stinkbeetle, "then we can meet and discuss this."

The afternoon held more discussions of the kinds of offices and duties. More articles were added until Mantis suggested a controversial Section.

"I propose," said Mantis, "that no person who denies the being of Spirit or future state of reward and punishment shall hold any office in the civil department in this Nation."

"No, no!" shouted Grasshopper, rubbing his legs at the same time. "We cannot require that, especially the reward part."

"How many of you believe in Spirit?" asked Skunk.

Many people murmured.

"Looks like most or all," observed Grasshopper.

Skunk suggested replacing it with the right to freedom of choice for serving or recognizing Spirit.

The discussion lasted for a long time and got tied up with the requirements for education and elections. Finally, Stinkbeetle appointed a panel to address the Coyote question, including Otter, Skunk and Rattlesnake.

The panel broke off and met immediately. Otter spoke first to set the tone in defense of his friend, "Coyote is a fine animal, a crystal, like a diamond."

"More like a crystal of salt," muttered Rattlesnake.

"Coyote is the foe of false taste, corruption, bad faith," said Otter.

"More like the leading exponent of those things," said Rattlesnake.

"He ate my wife! I was his partner in business!" shouted Skunk. "Otter, he *killed you* for your pelt! What kind, what loyalty, do you think you have?"

"He apologized," said Otter, still embarrassed by the incident.

"He *apologized*!? Words. *Words*!"

The panel broke up quickly.

Later, on the other side of the stream, Skunk and Rattlesnake were approached by Mouse with a suggestion,

"Why should we listen to you?" asked Skunk.

"Humans and rodents have roughly the same number of genes," Mouse said obliquely.

"You have our attention," nodded Skunk.

"Coyote can be tricked, or killed for a long time, or removed from play for a long time. I know some people who want him to go away, also. Let me bring their support-people to you and then we can decide for yourself. What have you got to lose?" Mouse offered.

Still later, in the cloudy darkness of the prairie, the panel and Mouse—without Otter—decided on hiring two foreign hit tricksters, Tarasque, from France—he had the body of an ox, lion's head, 6 bear legs, a giant turtle shell and scorpion's tail—and Tikibalang, the famous man-horse trickster of the Philippines. Tikibalang pranced in and performed against some imaginary target with a series of kicks into the air, which clapped to fill in the vacuum caused by his speed. He sat down and smiled. Tarasque lumbered into the room and sat back on the edge of his gigantic brown shell; he yawned and his teeth glittered in a ray of light, as he flexed five of his short powerful legs—the sixth supported a heavy wicked tail. "I know that gung foo stuff, too, but I don't want to accidently crush any of you."

"We need to have an animal retired. Can you do it?" asked Rattlesnake.

Tikibalang gave a lightning ghost strike. Tarasque blew on a leg full of claws and asked, "You mean killed? Who?"

"Coyote. Removed for a long time will do. We can pay you a ton of grass and hay," Skunk offered.

"I think the prestige would be enough," said Tikibalang, demonstrating a backwards kick against a slow imaginary foe.

Mouse and the panel nodded approval silently. The famous killers were hired and given the scent of Coyote's dung to memorize. They nodded their acceptence silently and left immediately, like express trains in the night.

Deer Woman Kicks Up a Storm

Tikibalang followed Coyote to his mistress's home. He watched Coyote go in with a bouquet of chamomile and an Ipod.

He waited outside, only fretting when he heard screaming and kicking.

This went on for a while, starting and stopping.

Coyote came out with several bruises and walked gingerly away.

Tikibalang wanted to have fun first, maybe trick the trickster by tasting his girlfriend. He went in and saw the tawny body of Deer Woman.

He smiled; she smiled. He approached her with open arms; she approached him demurely.

They lay down and coupled, passionately, then she kicked him in his horse head and he died. Ignorance is a bad way to start any relationship, and she loved to kick afterwards. And, the more excited she got, the harder she kicked. But, it was hard on many lovers, as death tended to dampen their ardor.

She decided to save the body for Coyote's next visit, as an orderve, oeurdeurv, horderve, whatever—she didn't know Italian.

Deer Woman had kicked Coyote in the mouth, maybe loosened a tooth or two, and he was having a hard time chewing his mouse.

It was still half chewed under his paw, when he saw the giant walk over the hill. Seeing that head, with teeth bigger than his own limbs, and a wicked tail whipping quietly around, Coyote decided to be civil, "Hew! Can I offer you a mouse,"

"No, but maybe I can help you get a rabbit," offered the giant, who seemed friendly enough.

"I think I know where we can get nine or ten," Coyote said, "that should be a good snack for both of us." Although Coyote suspected that all the rabbits in this territory would not be enough for this chimera from China. He guessed that Tarasque, as he introduced himself, was slow, but he kept away from the head and tail anyway, as he lead the way to a rabbit's den.

Coyote offered to catch the first rabbit, choosing to be near the center of the warren. He offered it to T, who breathed it in. Coyote waited for the other to offer to catch the next one, but he did not. Coyote suggested that he could catch a few more, then they could switch.

After the next, Tarasque attacked, lunging for Coyote just as he was dragging the rabbit out of the hole. Coyote dodged rapidly to the right, using the Fox-move 'Taunting lug.' T responded with a 'Kicking dog' attack. As T started to turn, Coyote circled him with a 'Dust devil' move, until his six feet were tangled and the giant fell on his back in the soft, churned earth, rolling, grunting, striving to right himself, but failing as he worked further into the bowl of dirt.

Coyote issued the Fox-move 'Counting Coup' to encourage the other to work the massive body more deeply into the soil. He walked in back of the big head, a safe distance, and sat.

He started talking to T, who asked, "Are you going to torture me?"

Coyote smiled sweetly and said, "No, why would you think that? I am not *d*ungracious."

"They said you were evil, not only the root of all evil but the stem, leaves and flowers—in fact, primevil."

"Who is they?"

"I can't tell. It's part of the contract."

"How did you get the legs of a bear? Is that a good thing to have? Six legs?"

Tarasque told him much of his early development as a monster, then his adventures in France and China.

Coyote had experience tipping turtles and porcupines, even a few cows and birds. He asked, "What would you like to do next?"

"You mean after I kill you and get paid?"

"Or before, if you want to get a nice tan here in the sun."

Tarasque was not concerned. He curled the scorpion tail out of the Kansas sun. Flexed his muscles. He had never been on his back, but how hard could it be to get upright? His ox body and bear legs would protect him for a while. "See some of the Mississippi river I guess. Take a ride south."

"I was thinking of retiring to Florida," Coyote admitted, "Just too cold, here, too much work. I don't know why Rattlesnake has it in for me."

Tarasque breathed a sigh of relief, "So, you know. Hey, what is that?"

"I know now, thanks. And, that is a herd of Bison coming this way."

"Help me up, now, please!"

"Ask the head bison, if you can stop him. You know you look nice and level with the ground. The bison should not get spooked at all. Aren't those rabbits wizards at moving dirt."

Tarasque saw dust and more dust and thick dust, mixed with thunder, Then felt the thunder and the heavy hooves. The scorpion tail inconvenienced one buffalo and the bear legs hurt two, but the lion's head and the ox body ended up pounded nicely flat into the field.

Coyote celebrated his victory with quick unobserved Superiority Dance and started a song: "Ishkakolitai to ishkakolitai. Aaaha, *iiihi-hihihi*!"

Skunk was calm when he heard of the fates of the enforcers. He shrugged and said to Mouse, "Now what? Shall I smoke him myself?"

"Get Hydrus, crocodile-killing snake of the Nile, and Khimakha, the ugly bear-ape of Burma. Double the fee. Say how the others lost," Mouse said.

"Good idea. May take some time though," said Skunk.

Military-Educational Complex, Gods & Animals Plots

In different sites around Kansas, unknown to each other, three groups were discussing the coyote problem.

At a military planning center at Fort Leavenworth, near Kansas City, Gen. Maynard 'Mayonnaise' Malais was asking his officers: "Can't we just destroy Coyote with space lasers? What about space lasers? I want space lawyers, I mean, lasers!"

"Sorry, General, the laws of physics cannot be violated," stated Colonel Witmer 'Witless' Lester.

"Why not? We can exceed any speed limit on our roads. Just bend them a bit."

"We can try," Witless rolled his eyes.

"Look, get Major Skreeg on it. Any law can be violated with enough money or bribery—Never mind, we can hand it over to General ZB and the action team," said General 'Mayonnaise.'

Lieutenant Gamble and Corporal Paste just looked uncomfortable. Gamble decided to go to the toilet and ordered Paste to accompany him. He always had to urinate more when planning these high-risk things. And, it was always so noisy——*Kapluoop, plump ahh ohh!* When he put the toilet seat back down, as his wife Moreen had taught him, he noticed that there was a woman's face on the oak seat lid, "Hey Paste, look at this, I think it might be Madonna or some rock star!"

"You're right, I didn't see it this morning," noted Paste.

"You used an *officer's* rest room!?" Gamble asked, anger blossoming.

"Think, sir, it might be worth millions on Ebay, like that piece of toast with Elvis's face. I'll get a screwdriver."

"I'll go with you and commandeer one. Don't worry, I'll just jam the door shut." And the two raced for a tool.

When they returned in five minutes, the toilet seat lid was gone and one wet footprint headed towards the door.

A moment later, they heard a scream, and raced towards it, Paste pushing first. Two halls away they found Sergeant Draper, naked and limp on the floor.

"What happened?" demanded Gamble.

"She, she—" and Draper collapsed.

"A woman?" They asked simultaneously. A four-hour search turned up nothing, although Draper's uniform was found downtown next to an Xplus-size woman's store on 40th Street. They lost the trail at The Econo Lodge on North Main Street.

At the Gods' Masonic Lodge in Kansas City, Hank-Ra asked, "Can't we just buy Coyote? He seems to have a charmed life and a charming way with death. We could save a lot of time just accepting him and flattering him to death. It would only be lies—and all of us lie heroically already."

Gofor replied, "Humanity says the insults were just too great. A lesson has to be taught to Coyote."

"Killing him means he *won't* learn the lesson."

"Then, let others learn the lesson from the dog's demise. That ends the conversation," said Gofor.

"You know," said Media, "we don't have to go it alone. I hear a lot of humans and more than a few animals are trying to remove Coyote from the game. Maybe we could get Horse to act as a go-between and approach these fellow Coyote-haters. Horse is respected by animals and humans. Horse?"

"I have good reasons," said Horse, "but I worry about the precedent. I mean Coyote is a god, and maybe only other gods should remove a god."

Gofor answered for the mega-one: "We established that coyote was not a true god. He was not worshiped by humans, just used by real gods for instruction, like Job or Runa."

Humanity finally spoke, "I want a private army, a backup to the professional US Forces."

"But—" started Gofor.

"I know. It has been 400 years since private armies were purchased and equipped, not since the 1600s. It's time. Gofor, contact the Greywater people!"

"It's Brownwater, now."

Humanity lifted an eyebrow, "See if they can get some of the newest US weapons."

The Coyote Victims Anonymous (CVA) met in the field outside of Horton, west of the main street with its two-story brick buildings, between the city and the Kickapoo tribe with their Golden Eagle casino to the west, and only 12 miles from Coyote's stronghold outside of Powhattan.

Eagle said: "Coyote has to stop overkilling his prey, it is waste—"

"No, that's not the problem, he's over*billing* his prey. He's charging them to go free," corrected Cockroach. "It's absurd, he—"

"Cockroaches, you are pests, dregs, leftovers of evolution, dirty little things that hide in cracks and get wet and flee the light."

"Dirty? No, we are proof of evolution. We are smart and clean, we groom ourselves and each other, and keep aloof from common insects."

"Can't we just reason with Coyote? Ignore Coyote?" said Vulture.

"No, everything with Coyote is sex or food."

"Sex?" asked Rabbit.

Unexpectedly, the conversation at the CVA meeting turned and focused on sex. "Hey Ground Squirrel, how do you protect all those females from other males?" asked Rabbit.

Ground squirrel just smiled and nodded sideways.

"Come on spill it," demanded Rabbit.

"Well, it's simple. After I mate with one of the harem, I just plug her up so no one else can get in," explained Ground squirrel smugly.

"I wouldn't be so smug," said Mole, "any 'mating plug' that can be inserted can be removed." And, Mole pointed to his penis, with its spines, and said, "I think this thing could do the job."

"Yea, Mole is right," said Centipede, "You mammals are clever, but we centipedes are also clever. I just use one long sperm that fills her up completely."

"Really?" asked Rabbit.

"Really, that sperm cell is as long as me! It takes me days to recover from making that, you bet," Centipede said, finally happy for attention.

"Hey, we need to ask Monkey King what he does, next time he's here."

"Aw, he never shows up. He likes Coyote. And, I know the answer," said Rabbit, "He told me once: the secret is sheer volume, gallons and gallons of ..."

And the group never did get to figuring out how to remove Coyote, other than exhausting him by letting him mate with monkeys or bison.

Then, the conversation turned to aggressive mates. Scrubjay said he was cowed by his female, who defended the territory and initiated fights with other females to expand or defend territory. Wolf said that his alpha female will destroy the litter of a beta female.

Scrubjay said, "Maybe she does that to keep you linked to her."

And then the animals talked about suicidal sex and madness mating. Bee said, "Saw a drone once, picked to mate the Queen. Entered the Queen and his entire organ exploded, letting him fall off dead, an empty husk."

"That's nothing," said Forestspider, "I talked with a dying Orbweaver spider once. It was horrible. He had lost most of his body and legs and was lying under the web when I chanced upon him. I offered to bind him, but he said it was too late. Then he told me his story. He had snuck up on the object of his desire, who was hanging upside down in her web, her orifice pointing right at him. He tried to fix himself with his palp on her but as he slid off towards her head she grabbed him with her pinchers and he gave one mighty shove as she started tearing him apart. Those Orb weavers are cannibals!"

"Yea, those females are all like parasites on us males."

"Hey, that's slander," said Varroa, a parasite on Bee.

Start in Neutral OR *Acronyms Aweigh*

The General had assembled his tech team in a briefing room at Ft. Riley, so he could be close to his First Infantry Division. "Let's start. I need to know what we are going to employ and how we can counterattack our own weapons in case they fall into enemy hands."

"Paws, sir," corrected his aide.

"PAWS? They have PAWS? We may have to call it off and rethink the— What the—? Oh, never mind. Brickmyer, what you got?" asked Gen. Harry 'ZB' Potterzebie.

Dr. Hans Brickmyer said, "Everything is electronic now. We are developing systems to tap into a plane's digital system to know where you are at any time, how far the nearest airport is and how much fuel you have left on the plane. It's called Techno Winning Electric Energy Test Interceptor (TWEETI). But, also, it can be used so marshals can communicate independently. As they roam anywhere in the aircraft cabin, communicating securely and covertly with ground operations, cockpit crew, other onboard air marshals, and airline cabin crew as well as digital aircraft systems."

"And, what have we got for disrupting TWEETI?" asked Potterzebie.

Captain Surmoody stood up and answered, "We're developing systems to disrupt anything electronic, in case the enemy got their hands on Hans' project. We call it Scaled Inflicted Leveraged Violent Electrical Systems To Recover, SILVESTER. It works by delivering varying but predictable electrical pulses to inflict increasing levels of harm to it: To deny, degrade, damage or destroy."

"What about side effects?"Potterzebie asked, not really concerned.

"A few pacemakers, life support systems. Collaterals. But basically a soft bomb. It can unleash 2 billion watts in a flash or more—as much as the Hoover Dam generates in 24 hours. Capacitors discharge an energy pulse moving at the speed of light and impervious to bad weather-in front of the plane or missile as it nears its target. That pulse can destroy any electronics within 1,000 feet of the flash by short-circuiting internal electrical connections, thereby wrecking memory chips, ruining computer motherboards and generally screwing up electronic components not built to withstand such powerful surges. All gone."

"Siliguri, can you neutralize Silvester?" asked Potterzebie.

"Well, we're developing a system to destroy Silvesters in case they get in the wrong hands. It's a man-made lightning bolt mounted on a tank, BUTCH or Barbaric Urban Terrorist Class Hell, " said Captain Siliguri.

"You know, I think I saw that in Baghdad last April. A tank suddenly let loose a blinding stream of fire and lightning, engulfing a large passenger bus and three automobiles. Within seconds the bus had become semi-molten, sagging hot jello. Rapidly melted under this withering blast, shrinking until it was a twisted blob about the dimensions of a go-cart; the tire just fibers. Human bodies shriveled to the size of baby-cakes, cooked alive by the tank, what you call it? BUTCH? It's a fabulous weapon, I'm sure. What do we have to defeat that, Horsekiller?" asked Potterzebie.

"The BUGS, sir."
"And, what is that? Have I been briefed?"
"Yes, sir. The Basic Unlethal Gun Spray-ray also already in use in Iraq by us. Basically it sends a below-lethal directed-energy burst at people from a significant distance causing a burning sensation on the skin and forcing them to drop what they are doing and get out of the way of the beam of energy. It can be used to disperse crowds in war zones."
"What about the Warservers, Warfighters, I mean?"
"They have reflecting armor."
"How can we get around that, and the BUGS?"
"Sir, why are we always assuming that the enemy will get these weapons within a week after we use them?" asked Captain Horsekiller.
"Because they do! There are always traitors who will do anything, sell anything, even weapons and our own freedom, for money."
"Can't we just pay them first?" asked Horsekiller.
"We do, but it is never enough," General ZB leaned over and whispered to Frank Coffin, "By the way, do you have my last payment for hiring your company?"
Coffin winked and gave the General an envelope.
The general whispered to no one. 'This is different. This is to ensure the right company gets the contract to make freedom strong.'

"Sir?" asked Captain Horsekiller.
"Oh, yes, ahh. The Response?"
"Yes, sir, the WILE."
"Spell it out, I can't remember every goddammed acronym. Must be why they are called acronyms, they are acrid, acrostic."
"Warcraft Information Leveraging Expeditor. It works by disrupting …" Horsekiller saw the superior officer fade and skipped details. "Sometimes it's called the Ibomb. It's a soft, soft bomb with no equipment damage."
"Sounds vaguely familiar?"
"It's from a children's tel—"
Just then Surmoody kicked Horsekiller and wagged his finger. It might be bad to remind the general at this time that WILE was named after Wile Coyote.
"Collateral?" the general asked, cluelessly.
"Without helmets everyone's brain could become delusional."

"But?"

"That's what the Avatars are for sir. Everyone's mental state is stored in the M1L1E computer darabase and can be restored after battle."

"But, how will the soldiers learn from the battle?"

"We will, sir, and then teach them in training," Horsekiller explained.

"Okay, go on."

"They are light information pulses that penetrate the skull, calvarium and membranes to a depth of 3 centimeters. The information is sheathed in images of sex so that—"

"Sex? We are giving soldiers sex?"

"Not exactly sir, it's just a taste, I mean like jail bait, I mean fish bait. Once they take it the coating disintegrates and feelings of peace form."

"Peace!"

"Well, yes, to stop them using their Bugs sir."

"Okay, okay, continue."

"… They have to be on plains sir, to get close enough. Otherwise the carrier wave would fry their brains with the energy of delivery."

"Christ, can we stop the WILE, if we have to?"

"Yes, sir, with Daffy, sir," Captain Gaines said smugly.

"A duck? Cartoon? Who in the hell named these? A child?"

"Well, sir," Gaines started, "M1L1E the computer named them. She's still a little immature and playful."

"So, reprogram her. Didn't you disconnect the television feed?"

"No, sir. And Daffy is a Directed Alternate Flow Energy weapon that could be used to disrupt the air flow around a vehicle or plane that was flying low to the ground or could interfere with the electronics of the plane or even temporarily take control of the plane."

"Who provided that?"

"Northrop Grusome, it is on their web page."

"Web page! You mean any terrorist can see it!?" Potterzebie raged.

"Yes, sir, I suppose so, sir."

"Well, classify it super top secret! What if it fell into the wrong hands? It could take down a low flying small aircraft from the ground using a laser or directed energy pulse, drop it into a building or laboratory. My God, what is wrong with you people. Do I have to think of everything?!"

"No, sir. TWEETI could be used," said Brickmyer.

"No, Silvester would be more effective!" said Surmoody.

General Potterzebie watched as the scientists argued. It was like rock paper scissors. 'Maybe we should just go back to stones and spears,' Potterzebie thought. 'Back to water-boarding and pulling out fingernails. I think we have to realize that a car battery and a dental pick are very effective.

Although of course, you could not discount drugs!'

"You know, sir, ground squirrels have a secret weapon against rattlesnakes. The ground squirrel heats up its tail then waves it in the snake's face, which confuses the rattler, which has an infrared sensing organ for detecting small mammals; the squirrel images larger. We never knew that some mammals could ward off potential predators. We never looked at the interactions in other lights, you know, infrared or ultraviolet," said Horsekiller.

"You're saying we should puff up our tail so the enemy won't know where to strike?" asked Potterzebie.

"Just an idea, sir."

General Potterzebie wanted to hear about the Terrorist Reader as a way to collect information from brainwaves in order to detect their foes.

Dr. Heighbale explained, "Neuroscience offers a potential window into the minds of terrorists. By understanding how their weak brains operate, and cross-matching that with the universe of data, we might be better able to predict where an individual might be or to anticipate his behavior before he acts."

Col. Dentwater responded, "We all know that 'Psychology' is 'crucial' in its application to the 'human terrain,' the interaction of culture, groups, and people that can, for example, lead to military forces being treated as 'liberators' or as unwelcome 'invaders.' Psychology can manipulate groups so that insurgents, not U.S. forces, are seen by local civilians as the enemy. Psychology can determine which interrogation techniques will produce the most destructive results without alienating the local population or international allies. We can start simple, with sensors that monitor the activity of people to software that would guide the actions of military commanders in the field by taking social and psychological factors into account. We are funding you psychologists to develop 'a tool kit' that helps combat teams understand the cultural context in which they must operate. We want you to develop hand-held devices that cue soldiers to behave in culturally acceptable ways, or shock the hell out of the enemy, sort of a panSwiss army tool. Yes. Dr. Spinsore?"

"When I founded WWW (Warriors Without Weapons), I planned on introducing nonlethal weapons like gloves and passive denial systems, like 'SirEnder,' a slow ..." and Dr. Spinsore droned on until several lost consciousness. "I call it the Zen of War."

"How did you do that without government funding?" Col. Dentwater asked.

"From calendars and bake-sales mostly." Dentwater made several eye and hand motions, and 4 MPs removed Dr. Spinsore. Dentwater asked, "Dr. Heighbale, your thoughts."

"When I started the Terrorist Reader Army Program, I used the brainwaves from virtually every culture. Now I hear that the foe may be an animal? Correct?"

"Coyote," said Dentwater.

"You're joshing me? The Terrorist is a coyote? These weapons are all for a *coyote*? Wouldn't a dog trainer have been faster?"

"All Coyotes are terrorists, Dr, they have infiltrated every part of our neighborhoods. They slink, they lie, their bitches pump out pups."

Coyote had just finished terrorizing a family of mice. He started to lay down in the grass to nap, when he saw a familiar shape, he jumped, "Hey, who are you?"

"Coyote"

"No! I'm Coyote! Where are *you* from?" asked Coyote Prime.

"I was made and instantiated by C-Coyote. Call me ICoyote."

"But, he's an avatar. He can't make—why are you orange?"

"I have a different chemical base from you, more silicon, less carbon, but I am flesh, now. What does that make me, Son-of-avatar?" asked ICoyote.

"More like a *Ratava*. Something dangerous anyway."

"Dangerous? Why?"

"You're a copy of a copy. Think of the errors and mutations. It's a wonder you're alive," raved Coyote Prime.

"I don't see that as a problem. Evolution is speeded up in me. I'm the future!"

"But, you don't *evolve*, because no other genes were combined in making you."

"But, I am evolving because each environment is different."

"Unless you have a fatal error that gets expressed later."

"Like what?"

"Like *me*. Trusting me," Coyote said as he grabbed the neck of the Ratava and tried to break it and suffocate his strange orange mirror image.

Then he let go suddenly and walked away, shaking his head. Icoyote sat up and sighed. Better keep away from A-Coy for a while, until he could prove he was a good ally and could help Coyote defeat those who were trying to destroy him.

Information Deformation OR *Loki Finds Brigid*

"Information is everything. And that's bits and bytes. The Pentagon increasingly relies on information. We substitute electrons for armor. With enough information, it is armor," concluded Captain Gaines.

"Nonsense," said Gen. Potterzebie, "There can never be enough information to substitute for armor."

"We link everyone and know everything," said Gaines.

Dr. Heighbale interjected, "Maybe everything is linked, but unless or until you know the inside of everyone's brains, you cannot know when a terrorist is going to use a homemade bomb to blow up your equipment and soldiers."

"Not if we can get there first," said Dr. Brickmyer, "No, all we need is a deep dream program to get to them. Give them their hundred virgins in dreams. Tell them it is over. They won. We are just here as their servants."

"And, if the electricity failed and they woke up?" asked Gaines, "We cannot predict human behavior. We cannot control it. We cannot predict the future, we cannot control it! We cannot surround the country with a control field."

"Uh, we're talking about one coyote?" asked Col. Dentwater.

"Give the dog a bone. That should work," joked Gaines.

"Excuse me," said Dr. Heighbale, "We have a coyote psych project."

"We do?" asked Gaines, "How will we know if this Coyote psych project works?"

"Easy, sir, insectabots," said Heighbale, "Wireless flying-insect cyborg—a remote-controlled beetle. A six-legged biomechanical hybrid that can rise, hover, and fly on command, guided by a radio receiver that relays signals to electrodes connected to the insect's optic lobes and flight muscles. With the mind of a machine and the segmented body of an insect, this bug-bot is the perfect scout: inexpensive, expendable, and capable of surreptitious reconnaissance. The beetles are strong enough to carry useful payloads, such as a miniature camera. The Defense Advanced Research Projects Agency (DARPA), which funds this work, is also sponsoring research on ways to implant insects with machinery during early stages of their lives. Butterflies can fly thousands of miles without feeding; a cyborg version would be a good candidate for long-range missions. Perhaps caterpillars could be modified to grow into adults that look like regular butterflies but have embedded wires and electrodes, allowing humans to control their flight. Dragonflies, which can reach 45 miles per hour, might take on high-speed missions."

"Okay, lets get to the money. How much?" asked Col. Dentwater.

"$14 billion sir," stated Maj. Skreeg.

"So what are we getting for our money?" asked Dentwater.

"Hypersonic vehicles, laser technology, using information technology and neuroscience to combine human and machine on the battlefield, and employing sociology and psychobiology to combat terrorism," Skreeg listed, "as well as a few arrows, pet toys and bones."

"Okay, okay, we get it," said Col. Dentwater. "I say *Go!*"

On C-day, Col. Dentwater announced, "Maj. Skreeg, we cannot initiate the engagement at this time."

"Why sir? Is the enemy moving?" asked Maj. Skreeg.

"It's shredding day at Leavenworth, and I have to be there, and it's Jackie's birthday. I gave a dollar towards the cake from Safeway. I think we can afford to wait another day," judged Col. Dentwater.

Skreeg was not concerned, since he wanted to leave the base himself. He had tracked the mystery woman from the morning incident to *The Plaza* in Kansas City and wanted to confront her. At the entrance, he selected the best clothing store, Neiman-Ryan, and started there. He saw a pile of expenses dresses outside a Regal change-room door. He knocked on the door, "A moment your highness?" thinking flattery might work.

The woman who opened the door was buttoning a tight gold pant suit; a blue cape was thrown on the chair behind her. She seemed tall, but Skreeg noticed that it was more physical presence than height. It was the brightness of her eyes, not the loudness of her voice.

"May I talk with you for a moment?"

"Yes, let me collect my purchases and I'll meet you in the Food Court," she said, totally nonplussed.

Skreeg went and sat at Fillipo's pizza, but waved away a waiter with, "Order when my friend is here."

When she came out with two bags and sat down, Skreeg removed his face and revealed himself as Loki. "I'm not trying to arrest you or trap you," he intuited the things she might be sensitive to. "Can I get you tea or a soda?"

"We have met before, in Ireland. When were you there last?" she asked, swirling sugarless tea.

"Must have been at least 400 years ago. It was a vacation of sorts," said Loki. "Why did you come here?"

Although she was sure that Loki had visited her island for looting and rape, she answered simply, "To challenge the strongest shaman in the land."

"And?"

"It appears I lost the second round. I was trapped in an oak tree for—I don't know how long."

Loki just nodded, "How did you get out?"

"A crack formed in the grain."

Loki let her have some dignity, knowing the crack was in a toilet seat lid in an army base and she might not be grateful to be reminded of how many men's asses had pressed on her face over the years, "You must have been clever and strong to get out. How did it happen?"

"Let my guard down for a stupid dog that may have been a decent wizard."

"A dog?" Loki started, "not a Coyote?"

Brigid's face hardened making her look more like an old crow. "I ate Coyote, squeezed our his remains and scattered them."

Loki was sure that he recognized her, now.

She opened a spout of vitriol towards Wakanda. Loki listened attentively. His realized his desire for revenge paled next to hers. He mentioned that Coyote came back to life, and she screamed, "*Ayehuuhhhh!*" Mall profits fell 17 percent that day.

Later, more composed and calm, Brigid said, "We need to separate and get this done."

"What about a rest first," suggested Loki. He gathered her up and carried her off to the Hotel Concordia. She let herself be carried for a moment, thinking, 'I can stop this at any time,' her confidence supported by her ability to kill any animal, human or god she wanted to.

Later, they did separate. Loki put on the Skreeg mask and went back to use the military technology to track Coyote. Brigid went to follow the social connections. She was able to track Monkey by the trail of ruined parties and violated housewives of Salina and Wichita. One night at a Political Party for Marl Everwon, a candidate for the Second District, she approached Monkey King. His back was to her, but his hands had found the mounds on a backside of a woman on either side. She tapped the shoulder of his pin-striped jacket. "I think I know you. Are you the famous Monkey King?"

"I have that honor," he said, farting moistly.

"I can give you more power," offered Brigid.

"And what would I have to trade?"

"Just that dog that left, or his bitch."

"You act like Royal-quente-ty. Should I prostrate myself?" Monkey asked.

"If you wish, but I propose a simple trade."

"Sik jiu, hooker."

"I am not famil—"

"It simply means eat a banana, or some crude flesh substitute," and Monkey waggled his hips crudely.

"Do not risk *ever* getting in my way," Brigid said and changed into a Horse and galloped off.

Wukong wondered how powerful she really was and if he would ever have to respond to her. He could always hit her on the head with his staff, now that he was reunited with it.

"I just want tanks and missiles," whined Gen Potterzebie.

"Satellites, sir." Said Capt. Surmoody.

"Okay, a few satellites, maybe the sniper guns and arrows, but let's get it right this time. Another defeat by the terrorist animals will ruin our reputation," fumed Potterzebie.

"Nobody knows about the first three, sir."

"Three! Shit. I thought it was only one." And General ZB continued his laundry list of lethal hardware, "And, I want it place by tomorrow, 0400. It's time!"

Coyote decided to go high-tech in this fight. Rabbit helped him design a tank, which they got Beaver to engineer and build. Beaver started with an old septic tank, but was unable to attach an engine or wheels, yet. Rabbit browbeat Coyote into wearing a tank suit from the Farmers Union store.

Coyote said, "Okay, if that's part of the uniform, I'll wear it, but I need a gun or knife or something."

"Wait," said Beaver, "let's roll it up the hill so I can work on it."

The three of them were able to get it there, but Rabbit's arm punched through a weak spot and was cut.

"You're going to need a shot for that," said Beaver, "it was rusty and had old human dung on it." Then, he cut down a few trees by the stream and dragged them uphill, where they wedged them on the lower side of the tank.

"What about a periscope?" asked Coyote.

Beaver smiled and said, "It was going to be a surprise," and gave Coyote long iron pipe with two angles.

Coyote went in and tried it. He shouted out, "All I can see is light!"

Beaver said, "I haven't put the mirrors in yet."

Coyote muttered, "We could have stolen a real one from the National Guard. Where's the gun barrel?"

"This pipe here," said Beaver. "Just stick it in this hole, *walla*!"

"And, this bur here?"

"Don't *touch* that! It's Ant's seat. He wants to be the gunner."

"What's he going to shoot? Miniature paperwads?" Coyote asked, beginning to have grave reservations about his weapon.

Coyote thumped the side of the tank. The hollow gong sound initiated rapid *gunfire* from somewhere.

Rabbit shouted, "*Beaver*, get to the stream!" as he rapidly dug a fox hole.

Coyote dived behind the tank on the uphill side.

The Army First Infantry had been keeping track of Coyote's movements with satellites and TWEETI-controlled spy planes with infrared detectors. Soldiers had moved into place the night before and dug their own fox holes.

Coyote shouted to Rabbit, "Corporal, are you *okay*!? Can you get a message to Ant, Woodchuck and the other animals?"

"First of all," Rabbit replied from close by, "I'm a Lieutenant. Second, you ate Woodchuck, and yes, I'll set Operation Trapdoor into effect!" Lt. Rabbit ran helter skelter down to a copse of trees by the stream, where the team was waiting.

Sometimes Coyote felt like a tiny particle being bounced from place to place by forces out of his control. No one direction, no constant, just a bubbling up down across in or out. His life was like a Drunkard's Walk. The military, church, scientists, hunters, ingrate angry animals—all pushing him. What did he ever do to any of them? Other than eating them or tricking them, that was. He shouted, "Get Frog a tongue-clicker laser!"

Skip and Buffy were in their fox holes waiting for the signal, when the bottoms dropped out and they fell to a smaller hole that trapped their arms and legs. All they could do was tongue-click their communicators, but then they heard the sounds of others being trapped.

"Something happened, I can't move!"

"Identify yourself!"

"Hey, someone get me outa here!"

Badger squeaked to Fox, "Shall we cover them up?"

"No time," Fox replied, "Get over to Operation Coolaid!"

The Infantry had brought up the Silvester weapon and focused it on the tank. The declining gunfire however had knocked the last of the Beaver sticks away—*Screeawk!*—and the tank rolled downhill and knocked over the Silvester weapon, which turned on some of the support unit, vaporizing them.

The animals had dug a large trap, so when the BUTCH weapon was rolled up, it sank deep into the ground. Since it was helpless, the entire sequence of Bugs, WILE, and Daffy was suspended, since each was tuned to respond from an attack by the former.

A WhiteHawk Helicopter dropped a bomb on the Septic tank, reducing it to rust piles. Flying shrapnel killed demigod Sports.

With the tank gone, Coyote rolled on the other side of the hill for protection. In the distance, he saw a strange box on treads coming towards him. He heard a squawking on his wrist computer and saw D-Coyote addressing him, "—sending help. ICoyote should be there soon. That box headed towards you is *Robo militrans,* an AI, an artificial, intelligent machine programmed to kill. He is sophisticated and can erase you. I cannot access his orders, but try to avoid him at all costs. Out. D-Coy."

'AI?' thought Coyote, 'Artificial Insemination? What if he wants to—' but, he, *Canis pragmaticus,* knew that he had to face a new mechanical species, a weapons-grade artificial species. Coyote knew he could not control the military systems, or even figure them out, but he could dance with them. If he could dance with mice or deer, then he could dance with machines. He started by paying attention, then participating in the flow, by heading directly towards *Robmil*, and greeting him, "Hello fellow predator, I've always respected your emotions and sensitivity, not to mention your independence and judgment."

"I have orders to eliminate you," announced Robmil.

"Why bother troubling yourself if I'm going to eliminate myself."

"Pardon me? What do you mean?" asked Robmil.

"I'm retiring soon, in fact right now." Coyote took off his Rod Steiger mask and became a Coyote, resisting the temptation to express some Dire size; he wanted to seem smaller and helpless to Robmil.

"They require video and a body for proof of kill."

"Are you transmitting now?"

"Yes, but I'm turning it off to privatize our conversation."

Coyote understood feedback; it was an important part of any dance. He dramatically turned off his wrist computer. "You could kill me, but I'm immortal."

"I'm immortal, too; any part can be replaced."

"Even your brain, memories, soul?" Coyote asked. "Why not wait 15 minutes and see what happens to me? If I survive, then we can dance?"

"Sounds reasonable. I'll watch," agreed Robmil.

Humanity was receiving feedback from her demis, Wrestler and Gambler, "Where is Greywater? Why aren't they attacking?" she demanded.

"They changed their name again; it's Zu now. They want to negotiate a new deal, due to the strategic complications from all the new players," said Gambler. "Do you agree?"

"No, I'm going to sue them, if they don't start shooting."

"They were going to use flamethrowers."

"I don't care, light a fire under them!"

The Zu commander had targeted Coyote after he left *Robo militrans* and fired their newly appropriated BUGS to stun Coyote so they could sell him to the Terropen Labs. This reactivated the Army's WILE, which correctly assessed the use of a stolen weapon, and fired. Soon, the Zu troops were filled with delusions of a peaceful nature and decided on a picnic by the river.

Coyote lay on the grass, twitching slowly, and then lying still.

The lone working insectabot detected another Coyote coming over the opposite hill and informed targeting.

Targeting noticed that it was orange but the shape was right, so it blew it to smithereens. Icoyote, the ratava of C-Coyote, was dead, before he even had caught a mouse or gotten laid; the real world was more dangerous than the digital, and he did not have the restart potential of Coyote, or A-Coyote. Unbeknownst to anyone, C-coyote had transferred his entire pattern back into the flesh without a backup, and was truly, irrevocably dead.

The Big Red One command was notified that Coyote had been terminated, so they sent soldiers out to retrieve those caught in foxholes.

Badger, Fox and the rest of Team Omega were sipping coolaid in iced glasses under a tree by the river, having interpreted Coyote's quick instructions to mean take a break to recover their strength between tactics, not to recover the broken weapons of the strong attackers.

Meanwhile, Gaia infiltrated the Gods' headquarters with her supporters, Nature, Weather, and many others.

"Get your troupe of *traitors* out of here!" screamed Humanity, who could only watch as her favorites were put in straightjackets.

Gaia spoke to Humanity and the other demis, "You henchgods, you will be disciplined, you will find your place and cultivate it peacefully or you will be mortalized. Humanity, you are big and you will always be big, but you need to diet for a decade or two, so other species can grow and make their places. Coyote will be admitted to the Council—"

"If he *lives*," sneered Humanity, "did you see what happened to him?"

All eyes turned to the large, flat monitor between the columns on the wall. Coyote had started to get up, unsteadily—he seemed to be growing to dire size—when he was pierced by an arrow, then another arrow—*Thunk wunk pft pfft*—jerked a few times, then fell again. The Infantry bow-snipers, Biff and Ked, stood up and cheered, slapping each others hands.

Gaia said, "I doubt if that slows him down."
Hank-Ra discretely changed sides, as did Celebrity, Bottomline, and others.

On the monitor, Biff screamed, "It's a Big Red One!" As Seth charged over the hill and tore the still Coyote into pieces, screaming, "Stay dead!"

Just then, Loki and Brigid drove up from the flats in a weapons carrier with flamethrowers. They got out slowly and motioned to each other, then flash-fried Coyote parts into smoking lumps. Brigid fell into Loki's arms and accepted an equally hot kiss from him.

Then Loki and Brigid stood straight and signaled Horse and Mountain Lion, who gathered the lumps, put them in a grinder, mixed the dust with metal shot and had the ball fired out of a DreK cannon.

The CVA members, the Gods, and the Army all watched as the ball disintegrated as it flew, arcing high over the stream in the distance, sparks falling the whole time.

Fox wondered where Wakanda was or if she had some Coyote hairs somewhere.

Ked asked Seth if he wanted to be part of his Big Red One unit. Biff was telling Kick that a bow and arrow could be very effective in the right circumstances. Kick said, "Player and me just put two bullet holes near the heart—you saw the two jerks. Rerun the video."

Loki and Brigid walked away hand in hand, heading back to the Warehouse of the Gods and their second surprise of the day—straightjackets and a change in status.

Gaia announced sadly, "We'll leave an empty pedestal in his name."

"For Sports?" asked Celebrity.

"No, Coyote. Wrestling can take over for Sports," she sighed and looked at the groups of gods, some restrained by cloth and others unrestrained by pleasure. Still mixed, so different, so uncontrollable—

Hank-Ra bowed slightly and said, "Have you heard my theory about the six waves of gods?"

Early
in the
battle

Profane Eruption

Well, there was no real victory. Weapons were tested, men and women were tested. Some were killed and laid to rest, in prime burrowing land. Two coyotes had been killed. New partnerships were formed. Most of the animals, except Fox, went back to their niches. Some gods returned home, others joined in the Pantheon at the Masonic Lodge in Wichita to plan their futures. Some of neighbors who witnessed the struggle were amused by it, since they thought it was for making an entertaining movie. Others became thoughtful and decided to participate in peace movements or the Peace Corps.

Fox lay down to sleep in the hollow under an oak tree. His dream song created a landscape of memory, so that when he was there, he knew where he was and thus who he was. The journey home was a struggle, but he got there, and wept from relief when he understood that was all the place ever was, in his imagination.

Suddenly Coyote erupted from the ground—*Kaploof!*—"*raaaaahhhhh*!! Fluctuation!"— Coyote shouted and ended up lying under Fox. Coyote rolled him over and said, "How did you find me? They shot me, tore apart me, burned me, blew me out of a gun, and scattered me. The pain was *d*ungodly!" Coyote squinted at Fox to see if he responded to the clever wordplay. No observable response.

"Some part of you must have landed here," Fox guessed. "Why not take a year off and relax, sleep, eat, sleep some more."

"Can't. Big projects, terrible responsibility."

"What? You're a carnivore. Just stay in the food chain."

"No, I'm an icon. Everything I do is critically important. Some see things as they are and say 'Why not?' I dream things that are not and say 'Why me?' Then I answer and say 'what a mess!'"

"You need to meditate."

"I need to evolve," replied Coyote.

"How did we get here?" mused Fox.

"Running for you, cannonball particles for me," said Coyote.

"I mean here, in the universe. Where are we going?"

"Waterhole," answered Coyote.

"No, I mean the universe. What does it all mean?"

"Sudden change."

"Huh?" asked Fox.

"Think about it. In the sun hydrogen fuses to helium in microseconds. That is sudden change."

"You need to be less serious. Laugh more."

"At what? Getting killed?"

"It *is* sort of amusing. *You* think of something funny."

"Okay, cancer is *so* stupid, it just makes the same thing over and over, no diversity, no uniqueness, just more of the same, and here's the funny part, when it is most successful at making more of itself, it dies as the host dies."

"That would be you?"

"Not quite as funny, but yes, it could be me."

"Look at this," said Fox, as he walked sideways then twirled and tripped, with his nose in the dirt.

Coyote laughed a little, then Fox started laughing. Then Coyote asked, "Who was that supposed to be?"

Fox laughed harder and said, "You!"

Coyote laughed harder until he was pounding the ground next to Fox, "I thought it was you on mushrooms!"

"Seriously, Coyote, ha ha ha ha, when you get too serious, just do a funny dance," urged Fox.

Coyote did the Drunk Human Dance and they both laughed harder.

Fox realized it was Hyena humor, laughing all the time at laughing. But then laughter was also an art and could lead to meditation. Or not.

Interamble: At the Dentist

Coyote was starting to develop some medical problems, perhaps from being killed so regularly. His bones ached. His fur itched. His muscles hurt. His head pounded, his teeth gave him pain. But, he was hungry and had to eat. "Ow wowowowow!" Coyote gasped. Something had crunched that seemed more like his teeth than the mouseburger under his paw.

"You should see a vet, with those teeth!" urged Wakanda.

Coyote grimaced—well, he had been grimacing for ten minutes lying in a chair. Outside the building window were other dentists in white coats flossing their teeth while they walked, holding signs in the crooks of their arms, signs that said 'Brush left to right only. It is the right way.'

Sideways hygiene, Coyote wondered.

The dentist came in, looking a lot like Steve Martin in the "Little Shop of Horrors" movie.

Coyote did not feel in the mood for humor, until the gas started flowing.

"Isn't that great?" Doctor Ryncholet asked, sniffing the air by the mask.

"You seem to have more canines and incisors than normal?"

Coyote looked up, with his mouth wedged open with equipment and blinked twice.

"I think we can fix this mess with six caps, a bridge and some braces, not the giant metal kind, but the invisible plastic aligners. For now, I'll just clean a few small areas of plaque and fill a few caries. Then we can make a series of appointments over the next eight months. What do you say?"

Coyote rolled his eyes and tapped a nail twice on the armrest.

"Make like your spitting, but the vacuum stick will suck it up. You'll want to favor that one cracked tooth until we can fix it. What about those Chiefs?"

"Who?"

Dr. M. cooled considerably. "How your teeth and gums respond to age depends on how well you've cared for them over the years. But even if you're meticulous about brushing and flossing, you may notice that your mouth feels drier and your gums have pulled back, what technically we call receded. Your teeth may darken slightly and become more brittle and easier to break. Most adults can keep their natural teeth throughout their lives. But with less saliva to wash away bacteria, your teeth and gums become slightly more vulnerable to decay and infection. If you've lost most or all of your natural teeth, you might use dentures or dental implants as a replacement. Some older adults experience dry mouth, what technically we call xerostomia, which can lead to tooth decay and infection. Dry mouth can also make speaking, swallowing and tasting difficult, and it can lead to oral cancer, which technically we call— Yeowwww! Ahhhhhhh!!"

Coyote had tuned out during the dental philosophy seminar, while the doctor talked and ran his fingers over Coyote's mouth. It reminded Coyote of live prey, and he bit down hard automatically.
The screams upset the other patients, all lined up in offices along the hall. They had assumed that the screams had come from a patient.

Coyote checked with the nurse on the way out, nursing his sore tooth.
   "Here is your complimentary toothbrush, mouthwash, and toothpaste. That will be $180 for the doctor and $50 for the supplies."

"I thought they were complimentary? What's the shitch?"

"They are, but we have to recover our costs. Did you just cuss at me?"

"Then they aren't complimentary. I am beyond crapprochament."

"That will be $230."

"I won't take the brush and stuff. Can I write a check?"

"But, you touched them?"

"Only the wrappers. I'll make the check to 'FArtistic Dental'?"

"We'll need to approve your credit. Do you have a local bank?"

   Coyote wrote the check in dung and left, without his complimentary brush and supplies, and without credit approval.

At the Doctors OR *The Tapeworm Diet*

Coyote realized that he had to see a doctor about a few other small problems, just to placate Wakanda. He loved Wakanda; she cared for him, she was frugal and a good mother, even though she disappeared often.

He told his story to Dr. Bucher: "I'm losing a little weight. My mate suggested that I have some tests to see if anything is wrong. What do you think? Is that normal?" Coyote asked.

Dr. Bucher leaned back in his office chair and fixed a pencil midrange in front of his face, as he answered, "Many people think being thin is healthy, but losing weight without trying is a sign that something is wrong. Weight loss could indicate a significant health problem, such as cancer, dementia, depression, heart failure, or malnutrition."

"Is that all?" Coyote sat up straight, which was hard in a soft chair.

"Well, weight loss isn't always disease related. You could be having difficulty finding the energy to cook, grasping the tools necessary to cook, or reading directions on food products. Age-related changes to your body could mean that nothing tastes as good as it used to."

Coyote was getting depressed. It had started with a few more wrinkles and gray hairs.

As if reading his mind, Dr. B. said, "Here's a list of the natural changes you can expect as you age. Over time, your heart muscle becomes less efficient, and has to work harder to pump the same amount of blood through your body. Your blood vessels lose elasticity. Hardened fatty deposits may form on the inner walls of your arteries. Your heart has to work even harder to pump blood through them. This can lead to high blood pressure."

Coyote sighed; he could have high blood pressure.

"But, that's not all. As you age, your bones shrink in size and density. One consequence is that you might become shorter. Gradual loss of density weakens your bones and makes them more susceptible to fracture. Muscles, tendons and joints generally lose some strength and flexibility as you age. Swallowing and the motions that automatically move digested food through your intestines slow down as you get older. The amount of surface area within your intestines diminishes slightly. The flow of secretions from your stomach, liver, pancreas and small intestine may decrease. You might notice more constipation. With age, your kidneys become less efficient in removing waste from your bloodstream. You might experience a loss of bladder control. Incontinence can be caused by a number of other health problems, such as obesity, frequent constipation and chronic cough. In older men, incontinence is sometimes caused by an enlarged prostate, which can block the urethra. This makes it difficult to empty your bladder and can cause small amounts of urine to leak."

Coyote was beginning to regret wearing his George Hamilton mask.

Dr. B. never paused as he stared at his pencil. "The number of neurons in your brain decreases with age, and your memory becomes less efficient. Although, in some areas of your brain, the number of connections between the cells increases. Your reflexes tend to become slower. You also tend to become less coordinated and may have difficulty with balance. With age, your eyes are less able to produce tears, your retinas thin, and your lenses gradually turn yellow and become less clear. Focusing on objects that are close up may become more difficult. Later, the colored portions of your eyes, the irises, stiffen, making your pupils less responsive. This can make it more difficult to adapt to different levels of light. Other changes to your lenses can make you sensitive to glare, which presents a problem when driving at night. Common conditions that affect aging eyes include cataracts, glaucoma and macular degeneration. Hearing loss is one of the most common conditions affecting adults who are middle-aged and older. Earwax buildup and various diseases can all affect your hearing—"

'Earwax disease?! How sad?' Coyote wondered.

"—age, your skin thins and becomes less elastic and more fragile. You'll likely notice that you bruise more easily. Decreased production of natural oils may make your skin drier and more wrinkled. Age spots can occur, and small growths called skin tags are more common. Your nails grow at about half the pace they once did. Your hair may gray and thin. In addition, you likely perspire less — making it harder to stay cool in high temperatures and putting you at increased risk of heat exhaustion and heat stroke. The most significant factor is solar exposure over the years. The more sun your skin has been exposed to, the more damaged it may be. Smoking adds to skin damage, such as wrinkles. Skin cancer also is a concern. Your risk of skin cancer increases as you age."

Coyote was sure it was cancer, now. He never perspired, though.

"Sleep needs change little throughout adulthood. If you need six hours of sleep nightly, chances are you'll always need six hours — give or take 30 minutes. However, as you age, you'll likely find that you sleep less soundly, meaning you'll need to spend more time in bed to get the same amount of sleep. Finally, as you age, maintaining a healthy weight may be more difficult. Your metabolism generally slows, meaning that your body burns fewer calories. Calories that were once used to meet your daily energy needs instead are stored as fat. Your level of activity may decrease, resulting in unwanted weight gain. Any questions?" Bucher asked, staring at the pencil.

"What about sex?" Coyote asked, really worried, now.

"With age, sexual needs, patterns and performance may change. Women's vaginas tend to shrink and narrow, and the walls become less elastic. Vaginal dryness is a problem. All of this can make sex painful. Impotence becomes more common in men as they age. Many men have difficulty getting or keeping an erection."

"Oh, no!" Coyote moaned.

"Let me ask more about your history and we'll give you a genital, I mean general check-up, get those vitals down." Dr. B. put down the pencil, then picked up a printed form, then picked up the pencil again, then sharpened it, then licked it. Coyote was fascinated by the ritual.

"Do you smoke?"

"No. Yes. Sort of. I mean three times a year for ceremonies requiring tobacco," explained Coyote.

"So, yes."

"Not exactly."

"I'll put down 'yes,' but light. Do you drink?"

"Yes. No, sort of. I mean I have fermented berries, and sometimes alcohol, for social purposes."

"I'll put down 'yes.' Do you eat a healthy diet full of fruits, vegetables and whole grains?"

"No. Yes, sort of. Mostly meat, but some grasses when I feel sick."

"I'll put down 'no.' Do you get exercise for at least 30 minutes most days of the week?"

"Yes! I must exercise 40 hours a week. Should I include sexercise in that?"

"If it's athletic and over 30 minutes. Do you get enough sleep so that you wake feeling rested?"

"Well, 's uslly uner thir mints."

"What?"

"Less than 30. Than 3. What do you want from me!? And, I sleep all the time, maybe 13 hours a day."

"Hmm, maybe you have narcolepsy. We'll do a test for that. Now, pull up your shirt and let's check that heart."

Coyote was fidgeting, trying to guess what disease he had.

Dr. Bucher kept saying 'Hmmm' and 'Aha.' Then he said, "Definitely high blood pressure. You'll have to have a scan to see if you have blockages in your arteries."

"I need drugs," Coyote begged. "Do you have a pill that would fix it?"

"Yes, I do," replied the doctor, flush from a visit from the Fresh Pharmacos of Philadelphia. "I think 'Spazac' is called for, but possibly 'Addictine' might be more effective; it comes in a chewing gum form. Just don't try to walk while you are taking it."

Coyote was not happy about the doctor visit. Maybe it was psychological, hey, he was immortal! He had seen an article on the 'Problems of Aging, Biological and Medical Aspects,' by a Professor Tawdry, where the good doctor wrote: "I have made a comprehensive exposition of the biological, medical, psychological, and sociological data bearing on the problems of aging to create valuable total impressions and stimulate new thought. I propose new avenues for investigation and new therapeutic goals. As a psychoanalyst who is better versed in the lore of Eros than the work of Thanatos, I suspect that biological problems, basically connected with the problems of growth, aging, and death, are futile—"

Coyote suspected it was futile. Maybe it was his spirit aging. Coyote decided to see a priest. Could the spirit age? Yes, it sure felt like it.

Coyote spent more time grazing with Bison, standing underneath Bison and eating grass, but careful when he heard Bison about to urinate. Apparently, Coyote had been hit by the old age truck.

A week later, he was invited back to Dr. Bucher's Office. Eventually, the Nurse said, "Doctor will see you," and led him into a maze apparently designed by Daedalus to imprison Dr. Minotaur.

Coyote slunk into Examining Room No. 7 and sat at the foot of an examination couch. After the ritual of the taking of the vital signs and the hearty 'Good morning, how are you' from the Dr., then the Dr. said "It's cancer, but it's a mouth cancer, a malignant melanoma, possibly from eating chemically treated wheat or poisoned food. I've only heard of it in dogs. It's going to require surgery, so we need to schedule something soon, depending on your insurance companies' own diagnosis and assessment. Stand over here and let me just take—Ahhhhh! *Ahhhh*!!"

Coyote had bitten the fingers as soon as they touched his teeth. He left to get a second opinion. The people in the waiting room put down their *Time* magazines and looked at the poor pained patient leaving.

Coyote meditated: Would his cancer be immortal? His cancer was him. It was just like him, independent, unwilling to be part of a team.

"That is poetic justice," said Badger.

"How can you say that! I'm *dying*."

"Everything dies."

"Not me, I'm immortal. I shouldn't have made fun of Cancer."

"Maybe, maybe not. Maybe even gods die eventually," Badger said, wondering how many other immortals were gone now.

Spiritual Healing OR *If Nothing Else Works Pray*

Coyote could not die! He was immortal. He was sure. He looked over at his coat of arms on the wall and read the Latin: '*Momento mori, sed non Coyotem*' Contemplating mortality, Coyote wondered if he was flawed.

Near a different stream in the prairie, Crow was talking about Coyote: "Spirit may be subtle, but Coyote is malicious. If it were up to Coyote, the priesthood would still be a male stronghold, guarding male gods from female interference—from women hyenas luring us with the fairness of their fur to sabotage the masculine philosophy in a masculine birth of time when men could storm the castle of nature in a united force and loot her stores."

The other crows cawed up a storm.

Badgera came to where Coyote moped and said she would pray for him to get better. He thanked her with a quick tumble in the grass. Just a while ago she was his favorite mistress. Now? He knew he had to heal himself. But, how? Meditate? Renew his religion and ask for followers to pray for him?

Coyote lay still for a long time, meditating on life. He received light and became enlightened. He received his prize and became apprised. He accepted his con and became conscious. He rejected his con and became unconscious.

He silently thanked Cedar and walked towards the donut shop on Main Street. Taking at seat at the middle of the bar, Coyote greeted the monk next to him. Over green tea and potato donuts, they exchanged thoughts.

"I'm sick of human separateness," Coyote commented.

"Humans are one species in a whole community," the Monk expressed.

Coyote answered: "Humans are different from other species and not as advanced as Coyotes, who domesticated humans to provide us, them, with food. Coyotes can become humans with masks, but a human in a mask is a fool pretending to be a bear."

"Huh? Yes, Coyotes?"

"Sorry, I meant humans can improve anything. We can add extra innings to the game, if you get me?" Coyote winked.

"I get you, but nature always bats last, you know," said Tipot.

"Teapot?" Coyote asked.

"It is pronounced 'tee-poe.' The earth is finite and this constrains our behavior, or it should."

"Oh, we can change when we have to, but why not wait, if things change anyway, but we're making a profit now? What do you believe, again?" Coyote asked.

"Taoism emphasizes the way of heaven, to be like water."

"You mean stay low, so no one notices you and chops off your head."

"That, too, is always good idea," agreed Tipot.

Coyote remembered his Mayan beginnings, and quoted them to his new friend, "Only the creator was in the water surrounded by light, hidden under green blue feathers, and was called Quetzal Serpent."

Tipot understood that Coyote had reached a position of altered consciousness, probably unreachable by many people, so he nodded silently.

Fox came in for a 'New York crème' donut and joined the conversation.

Coyote had just finished, "—the god of animals."

Fox said, "Animals used to be human gods, so humans should be the animals' gods."

"What about spirit?" Tipot asked.

"What about machines?" Fox asked, "Shouldn't they be the new gods?"

"Machines have no concept of heaven or the Happy Hunting grounds," Coyote replied.

"Where do women go? The Happy Gathering grounds?" Fox asked.

"I think we understand," said Tipot, "Even Great Spirit is part of Gaia. Think of spirit as a layer of air essence, within the atmosphere where all spirits exist simultaneously."

Coyote said, "I was thinking of starting my own religion, to be relevant in today's world: Consumerism. Think about it; just like religion, consumerism offers hope of a better world—but a world that we can see on teevee. The fleetingness of the new forces us to consider our own mortality. The vivaciousness of the new gives us hope, so we embrace consumerism to console ourselves with our place in the order of things."

"Perhaps that is a way to enter a simple life, then. Religion, Taoism or Islam, provides a context for us to transcend the everyday and to contemplate the other," said Tipot.

"The other Coyote, another way?" asked Fox.

"What is this Coyote?" asked Tipot finally.

"Only the greatest being. Approach Coyote with awe and dread," Coyote said and held up his strange new Dire claw—"I shall call you the 'unsubtle' claw."

"Religion provides a supportive social context, where people can practice restraint," explained Tipot.

"Exactly, which is why religion is declining. Consuming is much easier that restraint and immediately rewarding."

"But, that is the way of excess and waste," complained Tipot.

"But, waste is what allows sharing and change," countered Coyote.

"What kind of story is that? Waste? The big stories are how to understand the world, how to fit into it, to be bound to a common image—"

"And, isn't greed a common image? Gold?" asked Coyote.

Tipot continued, "A common community, where common rituals stimulate endorphins in the brain."

"I don't know these indoorkins," Coyote admitted. "But, the new global images of jeans and coke, they unite all people in a global community, and they out compete Wrongo-wrongo or what's 's name."

"Religion has the ability to open—" said Tipot.

"Science and religion are trapped in their old stories, which limit our possibilities and cannot admit a larger vision. It is time to incorporate new information, more knowledge and the wisdom of the best buyer," said Coyote.

"No," said Tipot, "Religion is needed."

"No, Consumerism," replied Coyote.

Fox said, "Tell me your myth, your image of god, and I can tell you your culture and politics. God the king? You have a monarchy. God the father? You have a religious state. God the con—"

Tipot responded, "The function of the powers running the universe is not to force obedience or punishment, it is to give and share."

"Who cares? The function of Consumerism is to share with those who have the price. Religious truth can never be proved, so why not make it a box of interesting lies?" asked Coyote facetiously. "If it is interesting, then people will want to repeat it and believe it."

"But, consumerism is a lie, an elitist, selfish lie, a lie to those who have already been beaten down and cheated."

Coyote did not reply. Maybe Teapot was right, but it took a lot of fun out of it.

"But if Consumerism were a religion," Coyote started again, "whose function was really to share better, you would admit it. It could have new awe-inspiring ceremonies for the people. We must have new wonderful rituals and rich ceremonies. I suggest the following rites of passage for everyone," Coyote paused dramatically, aware of Tipot's renewed interest.

"The First Credit Card; a ceremony presenting this rich plastic icon to tie future jobs to present purchases. A beautiful ceremony; the young girl sits on her white bedspread in suburbia and receives this magic item from her parents who are wearing their traditional outfits of seersucker suit and taffeta dress. One and a half other siblings look on expectantly. Beautiful.

Then there is the first Learner's Permit, the magic token to another, faster-moving, higher-status world ... Then the Popping of the Cherry in the Backseat.

The First Job ceremony. The Birth of the First Consumer clone ceremony. The first Layoff. Finally, Retirement and getting hit by the old age truck, often a double ceremony. How moving and dramatic would this be—getting a brass watch and a ticket to the old folks home. The ceremonial move to the assisted living facility with its graceful portico and chandeliered entrance with—"

"Are you a contrarian?" Tipot asked.

"Is Coyote a contrarian? No," Fox answered, "Although nothing gives him more pleasure to be on the opposite side of a good idea."

"Speak more of this new thing. What could it be called?" asked Tipot, afraid that it had already come to pass and would put price tags on everything.

"Pentacoyotlism, about the five masks of me, I mean god. It would offer simple answers for any problem, regardless if it was a global heat wave or simple cancer. It was the person's fault, some person, and it could be solved with donations to the church. It wouldn't be a blame game, just be cause and effect, with a simple assignment of fact," explained Coyote.

"It sounds shallow and narrow," said Tipot.

"It would meet my requirements for a deep meaningful quest in the world. That is, to grasp, to feel, to penetrate every secret in the world, to be part of every whole, to fondle the whole of every part!" exclaimed Coyote.

"Pay for my tea, please, I am a beggar," said Tipot.

Fox ordered some tea, as Tipot left. Fox watched people driving by.

"I'm worried about my legacy," said Coyote, "what can I leave to my pups when I fade away."

"Hey, nice euphemism," complimented Fox.

"Seriously, I am planning to die quickly after I get insurance for the pups, after I get pups, but how? I can't kill myself."

"Why not just insult a rigid religion," suggested Fox. "No good insulting Taoists or Shintoists. You have to go for the brittle ones, like Mormonism or Evangelicals, the ones that are too fragile to take criticism, and are required to respond with deadly violence. Boom, you're dead and the pups collect. I could jump over a body part later, or not."

"I just feel empty, sometimes," said Coyote. "The whole cosmos is nothing but empty and cold."

"Nonsense," said Fox, "it is warm and inviting, full of life, like this blanket on my seat. Look, you cannot see the fleas, but when you put the blanket on, you realize how full of life it is and how much this life is biting you and taking your hard-earned blood—*Ahhhhhh*!"

Part 5. Shambles

Wakanda Leaves 'n' Time OR *Vulture's Counterfitness*

Wakanda tried to go back 400,000 years, but she was unable to pull together enough threads to form a high-resolution world. The planet was right, but there were too few animals and plants. Even the weather was simple and calm. Wakanda saw information and patterns everywhere. They were what allowed her to partially reconstruct a rich past to live in, from the meander of a river to the layers of soil and where plants grew and animals moved.
She tried the future; same problem. She could still relax in recent times. Maybe she could just keep the time constant and go to a slightly different earth, where coyotes had become the dominant life form.
She could never tell Coyote about this. Who knew what he could do to destroy patterns, or chew on the fabric of space-time. Maybe Coyote was the Energy/Mass part of the fabric.

Coyote was playing with his penis, which not only had its original penis bone, but the server mechanism installed by Dr. Spicer's assistant. That was the problem, it wasn't working right. It tended to deploy instantly, which stretched the skin painfully. He needed to have them readjust it. Maybe he should have them take it out entirely and try some multiple-warhead unit.

Wakanda was wondering, as doubtless did many frustrated females, why males were necessary at all. Just a few sex cells, gametes, that was their part. She wondered if that referred to some kind of game. Males contributed so little, but that little was so necessary in most cases. And, Coyote displayed his bone far more often than was required to reach one egg. Perhaps because the costs of children were so low for him, but high for her as a female. Some radical feminists had suggested that males developed as parasites on females. Wakanda remembered that in some Chinese mythology, all humans developed from parasites on the body of Pangu. Hmmmm. So, she told Coyote that she was going backtime for a while. Not to wait for her.

Coyote was sad, but did not argue with her, because he was also relieved. This was a woman who scared him sometimes. She could do things he could not, and he was slightly afraid of her. She had been a good mate, but some time apart might be good for both of them. Especially for him.
Just then Vulture arrived to present his new new investment opportunities.
"Is this another counterfeit scheme?" Coyote asked.
"I don't like to use the word 'counterfeit' because we do not even make paper shares at all. We have been paperfree since 1973—that's ecological. And being paperfree means counterfeiting is not possible."
"What about these naked investment funds I heard about?" Coyote asked.

"I don't like to use the word 'naked' applied to funds because we do dress them up in fog, pretty bows and equations."

"Like credit-debt swaps? Isn't that where hard assets are replaced by formulas, such that: Investment = Zero assets + Promises + IOUs—huh?"

"That is an interesting way to look at it, but first I remind you that promises and IOUs are real forms of positive wealth; for instance, with an IOU, we might be able to give you a loan at a cheaper rate. This is not nothing, my friend; it is a positive savings," Vulture spoke smoothly and calmly. "Furthermore, those 'hard' assets are a real problem, like the hard energy path. Everything is soft these days. The soft paths are preferred and our schemes follow the ecological 'soft' paths," Vulture spoke coolly.

"What about naked short-selling, isn't that counterfeiting?"

"Short-selling," crooned Vulture, "is another traditional form from 1973. It is so simple. Say your company, Savage Coyote, borrows some stocks from the Bottom-feeder Brokerage House, who has shares in the Wounded Rabbit Company. You could borrow them and then sell the borrowed stocks. Then find and release some fake or real bad news about Rabbit's health. After the share prices tumbled catastrophically, you could then buy them back at the low price, and later sell at a higher price, profiting twice."

"Sound reasonable but not quite honest."

"It isn't about honesty. It's about fitness and efficiency."

"So, it's okay to double sell mortgages and triple sell stock shares?"

"Well, if it stimulates the economy and interest, it should be morally acceptable."

"Okay, put me down for $300."

"That's not enough to create wealth for you. I recommend $10,000 minimum."

"$400?" asked Coyote.

"See me when you are serious about earning," and Vulture flew off to offer Rabbit a chance at some shares of Sick Coyote LLC.

Midamble: *Retiring to Florida* OR *Cardboard Coyote*

'Welcome to Florida' the sign said. Having hummed all the way to the Georgian Atlantic, Coyote turned south and came upon a sign that said 'Florida Welcome Center.' Off Route 301, it was landscaped and clean, but deserted. No orange juice, no maps, just a place to lay in the shade, which Coyote did. 'They must not need tourists anymore,' He thought.

Coyote assembled a mask to get some food or a job. He could not part with the Hummer, so he hid it. Should have worked more on the mask. The sign company assumed he was a homeless drunk, but offered to pay him to carry cardboard. Coyote was standing by the pond letting the breeze ripple through his fur, looking regal and relaxed, when a bullet whizzed by, then the echo of the *bang* washed over him. He looked in the direction of the sound but otherwise did not move. He yawned and bowed his front legs as another bullet passed overhead. This echo was trailed by a string of curses. Coyote could see the little man in Bermuda shorts pressing the gunstock against his belly, trying to reload. Coyote trotted into the minijungle in back of the pond.

Squirrel shouted down from an oak tree, "That was the bravest thing I ever saw. That old fart got little Jackie last week. Blew him off the pole. Why did you do it?"

"Just working," Coyote answered.

Then squirrel noticed the sandwich board on the ground, '$99 dollar move-in special in Fiji villager.' "We're not in Fiji," Squirrel said, "This is Florida."

"How'd you know that?" Coyote asked.

"Google Maps. So, that's your work?"

"No actually this's my other job. The first one, they wanted me to put on a cardboard coyote to scare off the birds from the pond."

"Why?"

"Airport's down the road. Landing pattern is overhead."

With his first paycheck, Coyote was able to go to Bealls Outlet to buy some baggy shorts and a sports T-shirt that said 'Bucs.'

"*Hey*!" Coyote shouted at Fox, across University Boulevard, "are you following me?"

Fox trotted across the busy six lanes, "Yes, Wakanda gave me an advance."

"That's why?"

"Not completely. There's your entertainment value."

"I was afraid they found me here."

"Who's they?"

"Gods, military, animals, wronged husbands, the government, bankers, angry officials—"

"Sorry, I forgot. What we need to do. We need to gird the enemy in their loins," suggested Fox.

"What?" asked Coyote.

"We need to invade the closest military base and see what they have planned."

"If you say so."

"Think of it as a field trip. Still have the hummer?" asked Fox.

"Yep. Strange that no on seems to be looking for it."

"Probably too expensive to gas up, so they got a Prius with the insurance money. Let's go shopping," and Fox directed him to a sports store down the broad parkway.

"Why do we need all that stuff?"

"To fit in," said Fox as he handed a jug of water, rubber gloves and a respirator to Coyote. "I was there last month seeing if there was something from DARPA that I could use. Everyone I saw had these. Seems the water is bad, the walls are contaminated, and the air is moldy."

"That can happen on an air base? McDilbert? How?"

"Two words: Low bidder. I hear many bases are sick bases."

"Well, let's get it over with."

"We need Badger to get in."

"Why?"

"Badger? That's what he does—badges."

They did get through the gates and into several buildings. Each seemed generally abandoned, so Fox was able to use the computers to get information on the special computers, especially M1L1E. He also found several references to Operation Dead-dog and Operation Triple-dip. Coyote was reading the posted instructions, "Hey, these computers are supposed to be locked up."

"So were the buildings. Must be lunch time or quitting time."

"I think we should be going. I can feel the vibrations of activity from the other end of the building," said Badger.

"Okay, just a few more clicks here and I'll be done," and Fox took a DVD from the drive."

"What did you do?" asked Coyote.

"Nothing much, mostly got information, but left a few invisible ports in the program. For future visits."

Where are the Calusa OR *Casino Play?*

Coyote was depressed. There was so much junk and crap. Maybe the earth would fly out of orbit, become a wasteroid and crash into Mars. Humanity would be the waste disposal kings and the animals little more than a wasterisk on the human contract. Coyote realized that it was probably the view from western that was depressing, as all the crap floated in gyres in the oceans while the industrial shit—ship— of state floated on and higher.

Fox saw that depressed dog and suggested a drink. He led the way to a small cracker bar out of town. They parked the Hummer and went in.
"Hey, Meihada, go away!" shouted a tall red man.
"What did you say?"
"Means big shot," said the man.
"Means 'Big shit'" said Fox.
"It's all the same. I'm big stuff," said Coyote.
"No shit?" smiled Fox.
"Are you a Seminole?" Coyote asked.
"No, Calusa."
"How, I thought you were all moved to Cuba."
"Not all, a few of us get by eating gators and eggs."
"How?"
"No red man ever says 'how.' We *never* said 'how.'"
"All men here are red men, thanks to the sun. I am Coyote, you know, I can help you. What's your name?"
"Tequemapo."
"Sounds like an inquisition torture device. Coyote can help with that, too," Coyote said, loving the sound of his name.
"Coyote always made things worse," said a voice.
"Identify yourself," Coyote demanded.
"Don't have to, it's a dark corner in a dark, dumpy bar."
"So, you have an example?" Tequemapo the Calusa asked the dark voice.
"Yea, in Arizona, for the Tonoho O'odham people, Burden baskets used to walk by themselves, carrying their loads without complaining. But, Coyote made fun of them. Now they won't walk. We have to carry them."
"You're a long way from home."
"Yea, retired here. Seminoles let me play in the casino. My friend Holata."
"What's that mean?" Coyote asked.
"Alligator, I think," said Tequemapo.
"What else did Coyote do?" Coyote asked, after all, it was about him.

"Coyote spoiled the soup, ruined the beans. Talked out, now. Buy or fly."

"Just as I thought, no substance." Turning to the Calusa, Coyote said, "I can show you how to get pigs and deer. Interested?"

"Maybe," mulled Tequemapo.

"Over at Myakka Park, the contract for catching pigs is open. You could apply for it and get it, then give me a share."

"Spanish pigs, I know. Exotic animals did well here. I could eat Tilapia, but don't like the taste. Less work, though."

A young woman approached the table, "My name is Barbi Bear, what can I bring you to drink?"

"That's not your whole name is it?" Coyote asked.

Tequemapo said, "Bosomworth is her last name. A good traditional name actually."

"I'm not supposed to tell you my last name," but she flirted with Tequemapo. She was short and plump with black hair and green eyes, wearing deerskin.

Coyote had wandered over to the slot machines and started pulling levers.

Suddenly an elderly woman ran over and screamed, "My Machines! Get your own!" Threatening him with an aluminum cane.

Coyote retreated to the bar and ordered a Howling Dog.

Mare Rage OR *Trophy Mate*

Coyote was relaxing in the sun, on a big lawn in front of an empty house, lying on his back with his legs spread, listening to his stomach groan, but too comfortable to move.

Fox popped out of nowhere and said, "Hey Coyote, let's go celebrity hunting."

"You mean papparize them, with photos?"

"No, eat them. They're rich and lazy, so the meat should be marbled better, and they are dumb, so we shouldn't have to work!" said Fox. "Noisy meat but tender."

This was an expensive neighborhood in Sarasota, called 'Cortez Oaks' with winter homes for the conspicuous rich.

Fox cowered near the bushes, until a little yappy dog came out and yapped louder.

Coyote grabbed him from the side and silenced him with a bite and turn. As he was eating, he spit out a tag that said 'Baby Bit.' Fox wondered why it had to be told its name. Appropriate name though.

Then Coyote slunk along in a cowardly manner, and Fox got a Mexican Chihuahua dinner. The tag he spit out said, 'Prince Mince.'

Then a voice issued from the tag: "I detect this pet has been attacked! Please desist and step back!"

Fox took it and buried it. Coyote listened to the fresh dirt over it, as a tiny voice continued: "I am alerting the animals control police, now!" He scraped more dirt over it.

Squirrel came down and screamed at them, "That will be $10. This is my neighborhood and I am landlord."

Coyote talked to him, "Oh, Squirrel, great librarian of seeds and such, surely my money is no good here," as Fox played, until Fox was close enough to eat him.

"Well?" Coyote asked.

"Stringy, *puthooey*. We better leave, I see a bunch of shadowtails circling us, arrogant little rodents."

At that very moment Big Bob was being interviewed for KRTV: "Coyotes don't know the difference between their usual prey like squirrel and a pet family dog. It's not like they can read."

"What should be done?" asked Christina Wetherill, wondering if Bob found her attractive.

"Well," started Bob, automatically slicking down his cowlick, to present his best side, "You have to keep an eye on yur pets. Always have a plan, and the phone number of the Animal Control people. 555-5555."

Inside Coyote's cells, his genes were deliberately planning their whole dynastic future, with or without coyote's consciousness. Love, caring, altruism? Just devious stratagems to produce more genes in the bodies of the young females.

Thinking of gambling, Coyote realized he had to find a mate oriented to servitude, motherhood and pupdom. Coyote could not wait for Wakanda to return from the past, or future, or wherever whenever she was. He might be mortal, after all. He had to try to have more pups while he could.

He met with Netmaster Possum and got him to check out mates on the Internet. Squirrel prescreened a few then decided on Desyre, a one-year-old from Georgia. Possum created a prenuptial agreement and sent copies to both parties. He noticed that Desyre was much older than she claimed and had a bad case of rabies from a dog. He trusted that Coyote would not notice a few negatives as long as she was in heat.

Coyote was sure Possum was doing a bang-up job and was practicing for his bachelor party, when he saw a real cute Coyote cross Lockwood Ridge. He followed her, releasing just a few Dire gene odors and some Coyostenone pheromone from his tongue. He raced through a development to get ahead of her, then sauntered at a cross angle, spraying a few trees. Soon, she was following him back to his secret spot off the Tamiami Trail. He had to chase away a homeless man to get this prime spot between a dumpster and a block wall; it had a view of a stream on one side and an overgrown yard on the other.

He left a mouse by the entrance and backed off. Soon they were sniffing and exchanging vital information. She said her name was Utina, Timucua for 'Woman of my country,' and Coyote said his was Coyotl, Aztec for 'Son of the Moon.' Soon, they were hunting together, as he took her over to the Lakewood dog ranch.

He told Possum to set up the wedding. From experience he know better than to invite Crow or Badger. In fact, he suggested that they choose human masks, especially Otter and Fox, and have humans in the wedding party.

Then, the wedding day appeared. The lawn in back of the Beall's Outlet was festooned by mice and leaves hanging by their stems. The Bestman and Bridesmaid were Coyote's new Seminole friends, Hachi Wichi and Holata Shakingoinon. The Minister, Brett Blackhead, a homeless person from Delaware wintering nearby, gave a rousing sermon: "I don't know you, nothing about you. Looking around me, I need to tell you about the importance of having a vasectomy, to keep the human population within limits. You should be forgoing sex to keep your spiritual energy concentrated. Be loving, but chaste. Always cross the streets in the middle of traffic for safety. Never stop striving to get a roof overhead. To enjoy the sun, the breeze, the rain, keep your bodies chemical-free." He joined their hands—

slightly rough with longer nails, he noticed—together, and concluded, "Stay together just for the offspring and do not cheat promiscuously. By the powers invested in me by alcohol and delusions, I pronounce you 'Long-term Mates,'" and he released their hands to receive a bottle from Possum.

Holata caught the bouquet of ragweed and muhle grass.

A process server buttonholed Fox and said, "Itsayaya Jones, you are being sued by Jeb Burnbottom of Jebs Squirrel Farms for the malicious theft and mutilation of squirrels. This—"

"Oh, no. Not me. You just missed him—there he goes in the Green Austin Healey!" and Fox gave the young man Coyote's old Kansas address.

After the ceremony, and after the guests left for a pizza at Papa Nick's 13, as they were driving off with the convertible top down, Coyote wanted to establish his alphaness with his new mate and said, "Me Coyote, U-tina, ha, ha, ha," and laughed at his joke.

"Me squaw, you squashed," answered Utina.

'Oh, great, another smart woman,' he thought. Too bad she looked so good with a mouse in her mouth.

Suddenly, he slammed on the brakes, causing two other cars to swerve, as he saw a fresh road-kill Raccoon. He raced over and brought it back for his bride, who rubbed her head against it, as they drove off for a honeymoon at Gold Key Beach.

Over the next few days and months, clever words and promises came out of Coyote's mouth, then seeds came out of Coyote's producer, then pups came out of Utina. Then pups—the automatic penalty for pleasure. A new generation of pups, pretuned to the digital world and untuned to wild traditional coyote habits.

Reading the Comics

Utina wanted a better place than a hole in the ground to raise pups. She had taken quickly to masks and human lifestyles. All Coyote asked was that she could not become invisible or travel through time, which confused her. The happy couple had rented a condo in Bradenton off Cortez Road. Although it was a '55-plus age-restricted, deed-restricted, background-check, family-friendly, excellent community' Coyote was able to provide documents that proved he was that young; no one cared about Utina's age. They didn't have much furniture, being used to digging their own, but the neighbors were very generous and very curious. Each gift of a chair or table required a long, inventive lie from Coyote. Utina took to playing bridge and bingo Tuesday and Friday nights with the hens in the Community Center, which had a kitchen and a library as well. She wore her skunk-haired Elizabeth Taylor mask.

Coyote tried to hide in the condo whenever he could. He needed to relax after the stresses of medicine and marriage. He looked out the window and saw two of their neighbors talking in the parking lot, small Rekar from Serbia, dressed in matching golf shirt and Bermuda shorts, with black socks and black shoes, and Milo from Hungary, wearing the shorts, but little else, his large hairy chest and massive belly making him look like he was wearing a dark T-shirt. He overheard Rekar say, "I just have to spit all the time with this medicine."

Milo answered, "That's all? This Oxycodone stops me up completely—nothing comes out!"

"You need to take—" And they walked out of range. Coyote thought to join them for a political discussion, but decided to crank up the old PC Laptop that a neighbor Ryan had loaned him from his collection of six.

Within minutes, Coyote was online, visiting Shopper/jobber.com. "Because you can't shop without a job and jobs don't happen without shopping! And without shopping you won't want to live! Yes, it's that important. Sign up now. No entry fee." Coyote signed up. He went to Amazon to see if there were any new books or films on coyotes—it was so unfair that wolves were considered so much more charismatic and iconic than coyotes, who were so wildly successful at adapting to the modern age. Nothing new; someday he would right that wrong. But, he looked at photos of music albums by Aguilera, GaGa and the others. He wondered why they just didn't sing naked, like he did. Coyote was able to get a television signal through this computer and went directly to the wealth channel. Coyote noticed on TV certain accents were used on different channels or to peddle different images: Wealth TV was Brit accent. Music was illiterate rapper. Auto sales was cowboy/country. Lifestyle was southern drawl. He was distracted by the interior of just another well-appointed jet. It had leather chairs. He left it on, but got up out of his worn plastic chair, two legs dark with mildew.

He drifted over to the small stereo and turned on Neil Young, whom he suspected might be a coyote in a mask. 'Cowgirl in the Sand' started. He picked up last Sunday's paper, that Utina had thoughtfully left for him to take out to the recycling bin. The top page was editorials, mostly old people on socialized Medicare refusing to support socialized medicine for those without insurance. Huh. He found the comics.

"What are you reading?" Utina asked, coming out of the bedroom.

"The comics. Prince Valiant. What a strange comic. What a bizarre thing—no punchline, no jokes, just an endless story. Been going on for many decades, lifetimes even. I'm not sure I'm comfortable with a never-aging, immortal character trying to teach virtues to generation after generation of amused, befuddled readers."

"Coyote? Don't you think that you—"

"Yes? What?"

"Never mind."

Coyote read Doonsbury and went, "Huh, almost as funny as political,life." Then he looked for Robotman. No Robotman—must be a west coast comic, or extinct.

That comic reminded him of his last conversation with Fox. Fox had said, 'I think I understand humanity now. They think they are machines, living in a mechanical universe, able to replace any part or fix any component.'

'But, that's just a metaphor, like mother, father, or animal," suggested Coyote.

Fox looked at his friend, surprised when he remembered anything, and continued theorizing, 'They believe it literally, and the psychological implications are devastating to us. Rather than being mature, competitive or respecting of others, they try to take-over and perfect the other machines, which have no intrinsic value. Their machine beliefs are that everything is a resource; resources are unlimited; and their use must grow endlessly to survive. Worse, the purpose of the universe is just to supply resources; the purpose of humanity to consume—'

Coyote started to speak, but Fox talked over him, "Everything is driven by a clock, like a computer, which is why they love computers and cars with computers. Everything is warped to the machine and its need for fuel and flat places. And, machines give power, which overcomes ritual and increases damage. Thus, the machine people are immature and inflexible, unable to vary or change. Without the sacred, they are indifferent to Life—'

'But machines are sacred.' Coyote remembered saying.

'Because the concept of sacred has been reversed from the familiar, as it was for archaic peoples, to the unknown. Moderns made the familiar trivial and sacredness was bestowed on the unknown, like computers, wilderness or women.'

Coyote had responded, 'But, the machine is a hidden mystery that only the priests of tech—hmmm.'

'The idea of interchangeable units impoverishes everything, and lets humanity claim all consciousness and power.'

Coyote started to answer, but Fox continued, 'this leads to bad assumptions, such as mass production is the most efficient—'

Coyote jerked back to the present and took out the recycling. The curse of possessions required so much work. He was used to only working a two-hour day as a coyote. Huh? What happened?

New Brood of Pups OR *Last Viable Seeds*

Coyote had been so busy, he was not even sure when these pups had been born. He was surprised after what Dr. Spicer had told him about never having pups again. Maybe he wasn't so different. Or maybe they weren't his. His yellow eyes narrowed with suspicion. Their mother left every evening on her own hunts, or for some reason anyway.

"Dad, how come you gave us all the same name?" asked the middle pup.
        "I didn't. You, for instance, are seed3. Your brothers and sisters are seed1, seed2, seed4 and, oh, seed5," Coyote explained.
                                        "What does that mean?"
    "Those were the seeds that started you."
                                "Were there others?"
        "Yes, but Seeds 6 to 7,652,449 didn't make it."

"**Itsayaya,** I want the kids to have real names. Please do that so they won't go through life sounding like an ad for miraclegrow. Please," begged Utina.
        "Yes, I know, you're right. Seed1 is now Nekoti," and Coyote went on with the names and fake meanings. His mate did not recognize the Kickapoo names for 'one,' 'two'— "and Seed5 is Niananwi."
                                "Thank you. The pups will be much happier."
                        It turned out, though, that the middle three like being seeds and didn't use their new names.

"Dad, we want a pup?" asked Seed3.
                        "You *are* pups! Just take turns cleaning up each other."
                "No, a dog. Other kids have them."
                                "Other kids are human. They can't change. Just take turns putting each other on a leash."
        "That's not fair. Human kids have monkeys as pets, and they're primates."
                Coyote paused. That was a good argument. What should he do now? "Hey, why don't we look at other animals, like snakes and spiders? They make good pets. Let's wait and look around for a few days, and then decide."
                "Yea, we're getting a puppy!" cheered Seed3.
    "Don't jump the rump too soon," Coyote replied. "First, we have to work on our table manners."
                        Seed 2 rushed up and nosed the corner of Coyote's mouth and Coyote vomited up twenty partly-digested mice. "Wait!" he growled as the pups started to rush him. "Remember the rules: Rush in—do not allow others to go first. Then, gulp your food; get as much in as possible.

Always chew with your mouth open—"

"Why do we have to do that?" asked Niananwi.

Coyote held his right paw up and answered, "Because you have to be strong first. You have to breathe while you're eating. And, be sure to slouch as you eat to get better leverage on the bones. Also, waste a lot, since other scavengers depend on you for their meals."

"But, Mom—" started Niananwi.

"—was talking about eating as a human. Coyote style eating is different. We're teaching different styles, me and her. Now! *Go!*" And Coyote stepped back from the melee of feeding. When they were done, 30 seconds later, he said, "Clean up after yourselves. Time to learn to poop outside. Then, you can watch television in the den for 30 minutes. Then, it's bed time."

"**Mom**, we saw an alien!" screamed Seed2.

"Where?"

"On teevee. He was awful."

"What did he look like?"

"Gross. Human-shaped, but weird."

"Did it look like he was in a rubber factory when it blew up?"

"Yea, how did you know?"

"Star Trek. It was just a human with rubber on her face. Remember, if it walks and talks like a human, it is. A real alien would roll, flow or fly. Now, let's get ready for sleep."

Teaching the Pups Language

"Why isn't mom ever here?" asked Niananwi.

Coyote paused and wondered what he should say, then he spoke: "Your mother is an important healer. She is looking for ways to heal the other animals, especially males, so she has to go places sometimes."

"Are you a shaman?" she asked.

"No, it was too *s*hi-tech for me. I have to *s*hitch-hike on her coattails. I guess I'm just the *s*hitman of love."

Coyote was thinking about his friend, Monkey King. Whenever he did, he integrated copious profanity into his patter. But, he didn't want to copy Monkey's clever diacopes, so he invented new hybrid words by adding a single letter in front.

"Dad, don't do that," said Niananwi.

"Yea, instead, tell us how you met mom," urged Seed2, who refused to use his formal name.

"I first saw her standing on a hill. I said, 'I'm *c*hungry,' and she brought me a mouse. After that, well, we had immediate *c*rapport. In fact, our *c*rapture carried us to new heights of filthy love. Yea, it was *c*rapid, but—"

"Dad, stop doing that," asked Nekoti.

"We were married by Moronhawk, who spoke—"

"Is he a *c*raptor?"

"Ha, ha, good catch, Seed2," Coyote said, realizing this pup was fast, "and he is the most *c*rapacious of hunters, Moronhawk, plundering other birds prey—"

"A *s*hitler of birds?" Seed 3 asked.

"Good one, Seed3" Coyote was tired of being upstaged at word games, "and he said, uh, he—hey, look what time it is! Let's go hunting over at the mall!"

"Yea!" they cheered as one, except Niananwi.

"Don't you want to go, Seed5?" asked Coyote.

"Niananwi! No, I want to be an actress," as Greta Garbo's face flitted over her small features.

"Actors do nothing, they are nothing," Coyote said, "All they do is pretend to be someone else."

"But, that's all you do," she yipped righteously.

"No! I am the Trickster, certified by Spirit to protect humanity from—"

"So, you're a policeman."

"No, I am a hero, I only pretend so that I can teach humans—"

"So, you're a teacher."

"No, I have—" but Coyote abandoned his role as father for a second, as his guard hairs all stood and his teeth bared.

Niananwi assumed a submissive posture and turned her head to her sisters and brothers, mouthing the words, 'pretender, actor.'

Coyote realized that the pups did need to learn English, as well as Spanish and Chinese. His onomatomanic oneirotaxia was degrading their young minds. The pups were so cute at this age, he thought as he watch them race back to the table with Chicken O'nuggets.

"Hey, Dad, how did you name us?" asked Seed2.

"Yea, Itsayaya," repeated Niananwi, "How? Looks? Size?"

"Simple, I did not want you wasting your time fighting for a dominance hierarchy, so I just ordered you until you could get new names at maturity, when you pass to adulthood. These times require more than just food-getting smarts."

"In these times, humans get all their names at birth," noted Niananwi.

"Well, new times, nontraditional ways," repeated Coyote.

"Well, how did other animals get their names?" asked Seed4.

Coyote was surprised that the omega pup actually spoke, but answered, "Sometimes from the Great Spirit—Coyote, like Eagle, was a sought after name—but now days from their appearance. Sparrow means 'flutterer' and Mouse means 'thief.' Raven means 'noise-maker,' like Crow, and Owl means 'howler.'"

Niananwi whispered to Seed2, "Coyote was the last name left, so he had to take it. Tee hee."

"What about Tortoise?" asked Seed3.

"I think 'twisted legs."

"What about Rat?" "Porcupine" "Fox" "Can we see a Tortoise?" they chimed.

Coyote answered, "We can see a Tortoise tomorrow, I promise. Rat means 'gnawer.' Porcupine means 'prickly pig.' And Fox. Fox is special to me."

"Is he like your servant?" Niananwi asked.

Coyote shot a look of flames at her, unusual from that end of his body, but he answered quietly, "Fox and I have a special partnership that goes way back to Great Spirit enlisting us to help humanity from monsters. His name—"

"Now Humanity is the Monster," said Niananwi.

"Yes, more than you know, so we have to protect it from itself. The name fox means 'cunning,' if I remember. His brain is agile and fast. His legs let him dance to his prey, so they admire his grace, even as they are eaten. His pointy teeth let him slice and dice their meat. His bushy tail keeps him warm. His camouflage colors enable him to hide in plain sight."

"Sounds like you should have married him," Niananwi snickered.

In a flash Coyote had her young neck in his mouth and lifted her so she faced the other pups, "When you become parents, always lift the pups from the other side of the neck so you don't accidently choke them. Some parents kill their young, but coyotes cherish theirs," and he let her down gently, with an insincerely wicked smile. "Tomorrow, we'll find a tortoise."

That night, Coyote got out the scissors and pens and played with a new motto and Coat-of-Arms: Rays of light fanning over a sitting coyote, over the words: *Fiat latrans* or "Let there be Coyote" He admired it, wondering if he should add flames of light from under the tail. Then he reflected on his language, and wondered if the pups were right, and he should use less profanity. Maybe he could substitute other words, so that the phrase 'eat money, you profiting bank' would really mean 'eat shit, you fucking asshole." But, what word could he use for 'hell'? Suburb? Condo? Age-restricted apartment?

Coyote
teaching
the pups

Gatorland

After the usual stressful problems with pups who could make masks and wanted to act human, Coyote could relax a little.

Then one of the pups asked, "Where's mom?"

"Right here, dear." Said Utina, from the side of the room.

"Ahhhh!" Coyote jumped, "Stop doing that!"

"The pups heard me, except for Seed4, who takes after you, so I forgot to knock first, like you want."

"Okay," Coyote said, still irked at her for sneaking up on him. "Hey, the pups want to go to the zoo. I can't talk them out of it. Fox agreed to take them."

"These are exotic animals, dad, from all over the world," said Seed2.

"Okay, but let's go to a local area first, Myakka, and see the native animals, like tortoises and alligators."

Coyote was test-driving cars, a new one everyday, because he could, and the dealers would let him. This was the new Mazda RX-8, so they arrived in style and paid their $6 fee. They parked at the Upper Lake and walked to the observation deck. The pups ran back and forth in the mud as humans and then as coyotes and compared their tracks.

"Hey, what's that?" Coyote asked.

"It's a digital movie camera. Mom got it," said Seed3.

"Hey, when I said 'cameraderie,' I meant playing together. Let me see that."

Seed3 handed it to Coyote, who looked in the lens, pressed a few buttons and pretended to be filming, "Looks like fun. When I stir things up, I want you to be filming it! Okay?"

"You got it, dad, 'Chaoscamera' records all," agreed Seed3, whispering to Seed4, "I think we might have a close-up of Dad's bloodshot eye."

Coyote stood on the old dam and looked down stream. He saw a large alligator. A vulture was sitting on him and seven others seemed arranged around the body, which did not move. Maybe he was dead. Coyote wanted to look. He leaned forward.

One of the cute rangers in a green uniform said, "No swimming in the Lake!"

Coyote dove in. Underwater, he created the mask of a vulture. Bad idea, but the slow current took him right up to the gator, who was lying perfectly still. Coyote thought the gator was dead and the vultures were getting ready to dismember him. He hopped on the gator's nose. The gator suddenly opened his mouth and Coyote dove into the water. Not what he thought, so he composed a gator mask and swam slowly up to the old gator, 16 feet to Coyote's 5. Hey, pop-up eyes were cool.

He spoke to the old one, "Hey, gramps, how they floating?"

The old gator rolled his eyes and said nothing.

"I'm one of the new hatch, class of '08. Give me wisdom." Coyote said.

The old gator measured the young one and decided he would not fit in his mouth whole—still, it might be nice to try just to put these new competitors in their place. He opened his mouth a little.

"Can I bring you a fish?" Coyote offered. He chased Tilapia, finally caught one and took it back and put it, flapping in front of the broad snout.

The old gator did not move. Coyote was worried that the alligators were lazy. Not enough exercise. Maybe he could stir things up. He nipped the tail of the Old One and then barrel-rolled wildly in the river.

He saw Ranger Heather watching from the dam, so he charged her and she fell over the other way into the lake. The Old One slowly backed into the water and floated south downstream. Coyote snuck around the culvert and formed a Kenneth Branaugh mask. He saw his family helping the ranger to dry off, but figured it would be bad form to cop a feel or feel a cop. He waited until the ranger left confused, then said, "Hey, let's go see Tortoise."

They walked uphill a few feet until they were on an oak hammock in the piney flatwoods. They looked around the edges of the hammock until they found the tortoise burrow with prints leading in and out. It was large enough for Seed3 to crawl down to see that no one was home, except for some insects and lizards.

Coyote suggested, "Let's spread out and see if we can't find old Lefty."

Coyote saw an inviting saw-palmetto and sprayed all over it. Then he noticed a shadow between some trees and belly-crawled towards it. It was Blackbear, so consumed with honey lust that he did not see Coyote. Blackbear was rolling in the sand clutching a small hive. The bees sent 50,000 stingers to stop him, but they could not penetrate the fur, and only two found the sensitive nose. From a safe distance, Coyote asked if he could have some of the honey. Blackbear snuffed with surprise, rolling over, then he snuffed more aggressively, and Coyote correctly read the answer.

As he was strolling along, he heard a pup cry out. So he raced towards the sound. At first he thought the family was sitting around a dull-grey table, but it turned out to be Grandpa Gopher Tortoise, and they were feeding him tender shoots. Coyote looked at this antediluvian dinner in a shell and realized its only excitement would be being eaten, so it might not live too long past its prime. But, today was family day, so he watched until he fell asleep on the sand in the sun.

Zooland

The next day they drove a Subaru GT Spec B to the Naples Zoo. Coyote had never been this far south. They waited in the car, pushing buttons, until the Zoo opened, then paid a much higher entrance fee and went in. They heard another car drive up, but they were first in. Coyote and Utina walked slowly and the kids orbited actively around them.

"What's that?" asked Nekoti, pointing to a gazelle.

"It's a *d*ungulate," said Coyote, expanding, "a hoofed mammal that rolls in crap."

"It's a Dorcas gazelle, dear," said Utina.

"Dorkass," Coyote chuckled, with Seed4.

Seed2 said, "Ass."

"What's that?" asked Seed4, pointing to another cage.

"That *d*ungainly thing," started Coyote, "is a mutant dog sitting near his own crap. After nukular bombs were dropped on Africa—"

"No, kids," Utina said patiently, "that is a Spotted Hyena. It could crush you in his jaws, so don't get near. Your father is just being *d*ungracious."

"Is he *d*ungovernable, Mom?" asked Nekoti.

Coyote cringed at what Seed1 had said and for a moment looked like a hyena, as the hyena noticed.

As they walked by the edge of the monkey island, a spider monkey hit Coyote with a well-aimed glob of feces. Coyote's eyes turned brighter yellow as he started toward the monkey.

Nekoti grabbed his hand and said, "It's just a *d*unguent, dad, good for your skin."

Coyote smiled, but it was a terrible smile. He was tired of this *d*ungodly contest and trip. At least Niananwi was not speaking today.

He wandered off and saw Fox looking at a fossil, "Hey, it looks alive."

"It's a Fosa," Fox said, assuming that Coyote would misread the legend, "a cat with stubby legs."

Coyote nodded and waited for the inevitable clever comparison.

Fox continued, "I think I understand humans really well now. Look at these animals. Ripped out of their homes and put in cages to amuse little humans. They slowly go crazy, eat too much, try sex all the time, become more aggressive."

Fox paused thoughtfully.

Coyote made his own connection. "It's like academia. The aggressiveness is so high because the stakes are so low. Only instead of little bits of paper, these guys get little bits of space or food."

Fox looked at Coyote, surprised that his friend thought about more than food, sex, or crap. He put his paws on Coyote's shoulders. "That is what I realized about humans. They make their own zoos for themselves and call them cities. They become neurotic and obsessed with food and sex, and get fat and oversexed and aggressive. The city is a cage, an inescapable cage."

"Then why don't they destroy it?"

"Maybe caged animals try to break the cages. Murders and riots are attempts to break the cage."

"So, humans are paper-making machines caged in cities and trying to destroy the cage, even the larger cage of nature?" Coyote summed up. "I used to think of the city as a theater and life as a stage, for me of course. Now I think of the city as female. Anything female can be penetrated, he, he," Coyote appreciated his own joke.

"Not bad for an inattentive joker. Coyote, listen to me. Things will become hot and violent here. You must go north. Otherwise all your fur will fall out and you will start to sweat and bake. The weather is changing. Leave. Leave *now*!" and Fox turned and left.

Coyote stood still a while. Maybe Fox was right. He was always right. He was sensitive and true. He gave good advice, and he kept Coyote alive. So, what should he do? He just got here. He barely had time to retire and relax. Maybe he could stay a year or two without getting killed. Maybe he could move later. The sun was so nice now. A gentle breeze. Coyote fell asleep.

Nearby, a little girl said to another little girl, getting off the little train, "If you like this park, you should try Flalaland."

Flalaland

Coyote had overheard the little girls talking about Flalaland. He wanted
the pups to have the real Florida experience, fantasy. He was unaware,
however, that the evil Adolph Wittenschnegell had built Flalaland as part of
his scheme to bring real danger back into entertainment. Regularly, his tourist
Lodge burned down, killing a few inattentive people. One section had a real
Florida everglades wilderness, with rogue Seminoles who were willing to
torture a few tourists every year as part of their restitution. A few of the rides
had real alligators who were less tolerant of being poked than the fiberglass
gators and sometimes took a hand.

The family, with Fox, drove up in a Kia
Compartment. The entrance fee was now $90 a person but Coyote paid, as
business was booming. Unemployed people still had to look at porno and
drink cheap brainkiller booze.

"They anthropomorphize animals there," Fox said.
"So?" Coyote wondered.

"Don't you see? We are animorphizing humans in this book!"
"What book?"

"Oh, never mind. Camp-fire stories, then. The stories of you."

*"See? This is what is so silly, this constant reference to the book by the
characters in it, as if the author had no idea what she was doing," said
Hufferin.*

*"Aren't you forgetting that maybe the book writes itself through the
author without the complete consciousness of the author?" questioned Clerk.*

"Shouldn't we ask me yourselves?" asked Lopez.

"But, we're just figments," said Fears Horses, "you're real."

"Am I?" asked Lopez. "What if Coyote is writing it?"

"Who was that? What was that about?" asked Coyote.

"Just others telling stories about you," said Fox.
"I can tell my own stories about myself."

"Not really. You don't have
the distant perspective, the cultural contextualization."

"Nonsense. Watch: 'Coyote, that's me, as I say what I think, looked
at Flalaland and saw it for what it was, a project devoted to understanding the
legend of the wild Coyote as a themed adventure in a sanitized wilderness,
carefully constructed of saccharine repetitive ideas that show only the good
side of Coyote as he pretends to catch and eat the animals like Roadrunner,
but never succeeds, thus teaching young and naïve people that death is a
temporary inconvenience to finishing a life of adventure without danger or
responsibility. All this presented in an imaginary time where Whites were not
exterminating Reds—or Blacks or Yellows or Tans—

or the animals and plants they depended on, instead forcing them to become Christian farmers and herders who could be relied on to stay put and vote regularly for the Republicans, without becoming disorderly and drunk, without resenting and rebelling against close management by a minor department of a forgetful and mean cabinet in a forgetful and dishonest government in which they could not participate.' Yea, nailed it!"

"And this has *what* to do with Flalaland?" asked Fox.

"Don't you see? It's brainwashing! They are trying to reprogram history so it is nice. They are trying to sell us a nice profitable version of the past, of nature and wildness and other peoples who had to be replaced, exterminated and transformed to be useful for business and personal success. Of course, each part of Flalaland is decorated, on a base of plumbing and assembly-line efficiency, with the specially chosen characteristics of a chosen place and time. So, there is the magnificent 'Fountain of Youngness Park,' representing early Florida at the dawn of the Spanish conquest, with friendly immortal Calusa, thus appealing to the desire to live forever—"

"Why would you criticize that?" Fox asked.

"I can't live forever, just a very long time, as long as people say my name and include me in their thoughts. I just happened to have translated well to newer cultures. As I was saying, the Alligator lakes park is a nature theme preserve where guests can go on Safari and see 'actual wild' animals in their 'natural habitat.' Of course the original wetlands were destroyed and replumbed so that the water could be controlled better and pests could be removed. Ironically, it shows the human struggle against wilderness, the taming of another frontier, but also the amazing progress of the human technological experiment," Coyote summed up.

"The motto, I think, is 'Don't just look, Expose yourself!' said Fox.

"I like that!" exclaimed Coyote.

"You sound more and more like me everyday."

"The design of the Park convinces people it is the real Flalaland, although they never notice the missing risks and dangers—"

"Joe, edit out the rest of Coyote's harangue and emphasize the story line here. See that he gets some kudos and extra kibbles," said Yulalona.

"See, that's what I mean!" cried Hufferin. "She's regarding him as real as us. And, she is referring to herself. That's vanity—and that rhymes with profanity! Why do the characters have to talk blue? It—"

"What if she isn't real? What if Coyote or Spirit—"started Fears Horses.

"Joe, edit this out, so it doesn't look like I can't control my own characters."

Coyote heard voices again, but he just shook it off. Coyote walked towards the entrance, tongue hanging out as he looked at the Pacific Totem poles on either side of the Cracker Lodge. He went through the old oak doors of the rustic lodge and was welcomed by cool air-conditioning, over the cool native marble, past the native Hopi blanket hangings, to the old English bar fronting the waterfall surrounding the fireplace. Coyote had never realized the extent of Florida and how it seemed to be the source for all human traditions. Obviously, the Fantaseers had been at work recolonizing the past, as well as refining it and sanitizing it. At the bar he ordered an orange Fanta with Ouzo. As he watched the waterfall, the face of a large mouse appeared in the water, winked and disappeared. A god-mouse? Coyote wondered. The Realineers had been making the vision of the Fantaseers concrete so that he and the Junkanauts could explore this new realm.

The pups were sitting on the palmetto-frond chairs. When they were hungry, they found a restaurant, The Flalaland House—Fairly authentic food, with alligator soup and bird's nests. Fairly authentic waiters, with the broad cheeks and red skin of the first peoples.

Coyote asked for coke. "Its for the pecunious."
Fox commented, "But it's a global leveler."
"But it's a global classic brand icon," added Utina.
"But it makes you burp and rots your bones," said Niananwi.
"But it makes you cool," said Seed2, burping bubbles through his nose.

Coyote checked in and was led to his suite. He noticed that everything, every log, every plant, was made of textured painted concrete. Perhaps, there were no real trees and plants left in the area. In his suite there was an old gun above the fireplace. The bed was king-sized, just like the real settlers had. The pups started jumping and somersaulting on it. The bath had only a triple Jacuzzi symbolizing the privation and stress of roughing it, where only courage, determination and the gun could overcome the challenges of the cruel wilderness. Utina started the water. He took an authentic Styrofoam cup and had a drink of water.

The gun discharged—*Blamm!*—and a heavy beam fell on the vacated bed, *Boinggg! Carruunchh*! Coyote narrowed his eyes suspiciously, but decided to test his courage by taking a shower without testing the water first to see if it was hot. But, Utina jumped in first. Fox curled up on the floor by the window. Coyote had been impressed at the detail. Even the wooden wings of the painted butterflies were in sequence.

Outside, after an hour, the crew went on the swamp ride. Coyote saw alligators and birds, but he was not allowed to look closely or touch. When he threw a fish to one of the gators, the Guide screamed ' No!' they would have to clean it up before it rotted or got caught in the electromechanical jaws.

When Seed4 tried to pluck a flower from one of the water lilies, it unraveled part of the plant.

Soon, he and the family were escorted from the ride and told to return to their room for a lecture on visitorship.

In the room they listened to the television presence explain their sin:

"I am Emily, one of the Orienteers assigned to people to help them properly experience this Park. Before you can consume your experience of this virtual reality, you have to receive education about the selling of the stories about nature. Our Fantaseers have looked long and hard about the best way to present wilderness to all peoples of all cultures to maximize the goodness of their experiences. That is why we offer these state-of-the-art buildings, with advanced electronics and video production qualities as shown in our expert graphics. Now, please keep your hands and feet inside every red line. Please do not touch or hurt any of the displays—this will reduce the enjoyment of others, so please think of others. Now, be sure to visit the information kiosks on your floor, and stop at the Memento Shops for photos of you enjoying your adventures and at snack bars to make sure you have a balanced input of snack foods. Are there any questions?"

Coyote shook his head, forgetting the recent gun accident.

"Okay, the door will be unlocked and you will be free to enjoy the next ride after the Gatorland. That will be ancient Florida, after the ice age, when dire wolves and giant sloths roamed with bison and alligators. Thank you for patronizing Flalaland!"

That woke up Coyote, 'Dire wolves!' He had to see a dire wolf. He could barely tell his experiences were programmed to give him the most enjoyable commodity his money could buy!

The Dire wolf plastic model looked like a sick buffalo with gas.

"This doesn't exist," said Fox.

"Yea, but the fake is almost perfect. The surface is uncracked, the machinery is hidden. Why, a while ago I almost felt like I was defecating behind a tree and using leaves to clean up—"

"You were. That was the trail head, not the head head."

"What's next?" asked Coyote.

"Surfland. Or Tomorrorama," Said Utina.

When the money ran out, the coyotes ran out, leaving some oddly changed configurations. They never did hit the real Wittenschnegell traps, and so missed the really vital challenges of the park. Some others were drowned, electrocuted, crushed, and partially eaten just after the coyoteers left each exhibit. Coyote needed to rest at home from the stress of having fun.

Wittenschnegell had followed the Coyotes on camera and was angry that the timing had been delayed. So, he decided to bring danger to them—later, first he reset the frequency to shorter intervals to allow more tourists to experience more real Florida dangers.

Part 6. Rambles

Soaking the Blues OR ***Brownnosing***

Utina decided to tell the pups a Coyote story: "A long time ago Bluebird's feathers were a very dull ugly grey color. He lived near a lake with waters of the most unchanging delicate blue because no stream flowed in or out. Because the bird admired the blue water, he bathed in the lake four times every morning for four days, and every morning he sang: 'There the blue water lies. So I go in, and soon I will be blue.'

On the fifth morning he shed all his feathers and came out in bare skin, but on the sixth morning blue feathers came out of him.

All the while, Coyote had been watching the bird. He wanted to jump in and catch it for his dinner, but he was afraid of the blue water. But on the sixth morning, he said to Bluebird: 'How is it that all your ugly color has come out of your feathers, and now you are all blue and sprightly and beautiful? You are more beautiful than anything that flies in the air. I want to be a beautiful blue, too.'

'I went in four times,' replied Bluebird. And he then taught Coyote the song he had sung.

And so Coyote steeled his courage and jumped into the lake. For four mornings he did this, singing the song the Bluebird had taught him, he lost his fur the next day, and on the sixth day he turned as blue as the bird.

That made Coyote feel relieved. He was so proud to be a blue coyote that when he walked along, he looked about on every side to see if anyone noticed how fine and blue he was. Then he started running along very fast, looking at his shadow to see if it also was blue. He was not watching the road, and he tripped on a root that threw him down upon the ground and he became covered with dust. To this day all coyotes are the color of dust."

Coyote said, "That was *not* how it happened."

"Tell us your story," the pups begged.

"All right. I saw a naked bird, with no feathers, near a small lake. There was a hawk in the sky. The bird begged, 'Please protect me, and I'll tell you the secret of being blue.' I was a beautiful green, but considered maybe the blueness might help my daylight hunting skills. So, all day and night I stood guard over the bird, never flagging, never failing or falling asleep. That next morning his feathers were bright blue. To reward me, he told me the secret: 'Go in 4 days in a row and on the sixth you will be blue. But, he did not tell me everything. He did not tell me I had to dry the color first all morning. So, when I went off right away to show Mole, my first mate, the new colors. As I was walking along the road, I suddenly tripped over a yellow leg and my fur was coated with dust that stuck to the blue. I saw a blue flash in the sky, but could prove nothing. That is what really happened, he just wanted to keep his secrets," Coyote sniffed.

Utina said, "Nothing is always as it seems. There is a side to everything. So, I invited Fric tonight to tell his side of the story."

A beautiful mountain bluebird fluttered in and landed on a root above Utina's head, and exchanged glares with Coyote.

"I was there. I knew someone was stalking me for a week. Then I saw a vomit-green beast who grabbed me as I was drying my feathers, after the change from regal grey to wild two-tone blue. I was small and edible. When he harassed me and threatened to eat me unless I told him the secret, a secret we bluebirds had kept for millennia, that we had to go in the lake once a year—even our females were the bright blue as the males—I was terrified! What could I do? I told him what he asked, but not everything he needed to know. I was under duress. But, that made no difference. He tried to kill me on the sixth day. I had been under his claw for five days and nights, but I had dug a little and when he repositioned his fangy mouth, I leapt free and flew. He was so eager to kill me to keep his secret that he tripped and fell and rolled in the dirt. That is the truth."

Utina swallowed Bluebird whole. "There are many truths of course," she said, with her mouth full, giving Coyote a wing, "and we should respect all perspectives and the truths, while recognizing that family loyalty is more important than bald truth."

"And that is the origin of the blues," said Coyote. He gave some feathers to the pups to play with.

One of the pups, Seed3, whispered, "I heard that once bluebirds lent their feathers to Coyote so he could fly to top of a mesa. They climbed up, but then they had to take back the feathers so they could fly down. Coyote became impatient and tried to jump down, but got killed. The bluebirds brought him back to life."

"Do you think," said Seed4, sneezing first from his feather allergy, "that he remembers that they could bring him back to life now if he needed it?"

"No!" and they giggled quietly.

Penamble: What's on Teevee?

Coyote was more depressed. He was fatter, from beer and cheetoes. He was tired of the paper and sitting in front of the teevee, too settled to move, surrounded by crumbs and pieces of crap. He thought of a biological pun: This was fecesis, the establishment of an animal in its place. But, it wasn't funny enough to cheer him up. Coyote changed channels. It was Sunday morning at Eleven. He was hoping to see his favorite team, The Stealers, in action, but he forgotten about east coast time. He turned to channel 3; it was 'Dirty Jobs' but there was a commercial for some car, BMW—it was on an empty road going 90. Coyote looked at cars as free transportation, but the car companies presented them as priceless luxury sanctuaries. Then he turned to 'Wild Kingdom' but it was at commercial break; it was a giant grey hamburger, done 'your way.' 'My way is on the hoof,' thought Coyote.

The next channel was 'Real Housewives-Atlanta.' Coyote wanted to see that, but the channel had another car commercial, Ford this time, on the same empty road, perhaps in Nevada. Coyote flipped faster: The Sopranos, The Inspiration Ministry, Florida's Next Top Model, Rev. Ernest Angely, Monster Inside Me—Coyote stopped. This commercial was for Domino's Roasted Sandwiches, so Coyote phoned in his order. Then the program returned, but it really was not about monsters, as Coyote understood them, just silly fluff. He went to the next channel, which was paid programming for exercise equipment. He unconsciously moved back and forth entrained with the actor on the screen. He changed channels to 'Capitol,' which was now at commercial, appropriately enough for the program called, "Lie to Me." That was on Tuesday or something too far in the future for him. He switched to NFL Football Countdown, which was advertising a black cartoon family, the Clevelands. Then, Married with Children: "I'm not going any further, Peg!"

But, if 'Married' was on then 'Housewives' might be, if all programs were synchronized. So he started clicking backwards.

"He's in the red zone, Peter [click] —where he admitted lying about his mistress— look at him pump those— monsters trying to get out— of heaven where he lives now— walking dramatically down the runway— to beg forgiveness from Jesus, now— but he'll kill him, just like that, if— he tries to come onto me one more time— suffocating the poor female with that bite, those teeth— and we can just take this trash to the County Dump, now."

Coyote turned from 'Dirty Jobs' to the NFL Tailgate party. He realized then that Fox was right, humans were developing into separate species from each other, the linemen were amazing large mammals, like Moose, the defensive backfield were like wolves, the free safety was like a coyote, moving on his own, the tailbacks like rabbits, and the coaching staff were like bears before hibernation, fat, anxious and grumpy. Then he drifted to sleep again, and missed the 'Bones' on Thursday commercial.

Starting the E=MC² Bank

Crow carried a message from Great Spirit to Coyote: "You were chosen by Spirit to slay monsters that threaten humanity. You are done, now. You may go retire into the comforting mists of past gods and demi-beings."

"Love to," said Coyote. "Please give Spirit this message: 'But there are still monsters. The new Machine monsters that spew pollutions that can wreck the planet. The new Human monster that threatens all life with conversion to human flesh. The Bank monster that converts all wealth to electronic bank credits, which can disappear. I must slay these first.'"

"Poof, many of these 'monsters' are tiny and inconsequential. Carcinogens are feeble. Bacteria are weak," said Crow, "Spirit will not—"

"All of these are greater than you think, or appreciate. But, I expect no thanks. I will defeat them and go without thanks." And Coyote decided to start with toenail fungus.

Crow flew off, cawing his displeasure.

But, **the Bank** monster presented itself first, by doubling the fees in Coyote's account. An extra fee for depositing on line, one for using the bank tellers, another for using his cash card. This was ridiculous, Coyote thought, this legalized hoarding and then stealing. Coyote knew he could teach them a lesson by making a more prosperous bank, one not stupid enough to buy its own counterfeit fluff.

"I want to call it *Coyote* Bank!" shouted Coyote to his possible bizness partners.

"Bad idea," said Ant. "You have a bad rep, like Grasshopper, and unlike me and Bee, who are models of savings and thrift."

"So, you think humans are going to go to Bee bank or Ant bank?"

"What about an A&B Bank?" asked Bee.

"No! *Wait*!" said Coyote. "That's why we'll call it E=mc² bank. Listen to this: 'We're not your typical greedy stupid bank, like Walkoverya Bank or WashingMut Bank. We're a new bank, a smart bank, a bank for the brainy new century. E=mc² means 'Earnings equals materials multiplied by Creativity squared.' That's why you get 200 percent earnings in 20 years!' That should relax people. They want money handled by smart people, not idiots. And this is the bank of, with, by, and for smart people."

"Ah, I don't think—it should be for dumb people, too" started Bee.

Coyote continued: "*Yes*! Modern banks need modern language and modern approaches. Modern theories, but with anchors to real wealth and basic accountability to inspire trust."

Bee and Ant looked each other as Coyote tried to impress them with emotion, words and math.

"I think the equations are good," said Ant, "but solving the equations reveals the possibility of a complete collapse."

"Oh, poof, don't worry," Coyote assured Ant, "This combination of debtors defaulting in this combination could only happen once every 10,000 years. So, it'd a 10,000 year event. Yes. So, it could happen tomorrow? Yes, but then not again for 10,000 years."

"Or 3 years," said Bee, "the numbers you showed require a 46 million-year time frame. So, it could happen 990 years in a row. Unrealistic, even for a long-lived species."

"I thought we were talking about a smart, trustful community bank, that lent and borrowed small, secured amounts," said Ant.

"That was before I realized that we might be able sell this idea to the really large, government-loved banks," Coyote explained.

"But, it is fundamentally dishonest," concluded Bee.

"Well, the victims would be only dishonest, rich people."

"No, the trickle-down would dry up," Ant said, "I'm leaving."

Bee and Ant walked out of the deluxe rented office.

"Wait, maybe we could call it Ant-Bee—" Coyote started. But, he was too late. He leaned against a leather chair, as he was thinking, 'Maybe I should call the company Ameriprize? Nah!' He had to look for new backing. Maybe Vulture or Opossum.

Ant & Bee
Bank—or
$E=mc^2$
Bank?

Penamble: Shark on the Beach

Cars are a potent symbol of freedom, going by themselves on empty freeways, at most carrying a single person from the crowding of the city full of cars. The driver is liberated from any interference with others, from the sounds of the city as well as the noise of other unhappy, presumably carless, souls. The driver is omnipotent and can drive on grass, rocks and clouds. Everywhere. Coyote remembered the importance of symbols, as he drove the Prius to Coquina Beech. He parked in the lot near a picnic table. The pups ran out to play in the sand.

As Coyote was walking to the beach, an elderly woman raced by him and said, "Shark on Beach! Got to call animal control."

Coyote hurried to the Gulf water. Sure enough a shark had washed up in the surf. Coyote knew something about animal control and grabbed the tail to drag it back. He couldn't move it. We walked around to the head, careful to stay out of range of those teeth, "Hey, whas'up?"

"Dying."

"What happened?"

"Dolphin torpedoed me in the liver. Too close to her young I guess."

"You're pretty philosophical about it. You want me to avenge you?" Coyote asked.

"No, not her fault. Wrong place, wrong time. I just looked dangerous. That's life."

"You didn't smile did you?"

"Yea, how'd you know? Listen, it's getting dark."

"What can I do for you?"

"Bite that woman who ran to get the navy, would you? Thanks. Bye," and Shark stopped moving at all.

Coyote saluted the noble predator and went to sit on the beach with Utina. More people were coming up now. A few men tried to move the shark back in the water—too heavy. Then a Coast Guard boat came and put a winch on the tail. That didn't work, until they aimed the boat south a bit, then the shark slipped into the water. Coyote watched it until it was out of sight. Then, he and his mate picked up shells while the kids play in surf. He threw a shell back. Coyote thought, 'A shark cannot become vegetarian through an act of will. Shark is hungrier, Wolf is stronger, Ravens are smarter, but we coyotes are cleverer. We are more cautious, we are more sensitive. We can communicate and sing and dance to survive.' Maybe he should bite a lot of nastier, tastier humans for making shark fin soup.

Paradise College of Art and Banking Science

Back at the condo, Coyote decided to catch up on the web. He went through Firefox—what else?—and searched Dogpile—what else?—for the news of his beloved Koors College. Seemed Prez Kankersoar had run off with the money. The college was licensed but not accredited. Then it lost its state license under President Glurtus. Coyote was sad that his first foray into education, Koors College, had not worked. But, Coyote used it as a springboard to Presidential candidate for Central Southwest State College of Florida (CeSoStaCoFla).

When he met with the Moneybags, or Regents, he presented his foresighted ideas, "It's all art and money, these days. I know of a bank that can lend its expertise, a smart bank, where everyone has smartphones in their smartclothes and drives smartcars to work. It's the E=MC^2 bank. I think you'll be pleased. First we need to change this name to the Paradise College of Art and Banking Science. God, this is so exciting!"

The Regents readjusted their asses slowly, then one, the pithy Rothschild Carosel, said, "We need a slogan."

"I know, Path to Preeminence?" suggested Montel Hardy.

"No," replied Coyote, "how about 'Exit to Eminence'? We are past the 'Pre'-stage. Maybe 'Gateway to Greatness?' or 'Road to Repute?' Hmm, how about 'Sidewalk to Superiority? 'Course to Conspicuousness?' 'Driveway to Distinguishment?' or 'Freeway to Fundability'?"

"I like the gateway thingy. It should be Learner-centered," suggested Lesley O'Lariat.

"Oh no, no, income-centered," Coyote judged.

"What is our target?" asked Carosel.

"Money-bearers of course," said Coyote.

"Perhaps we could call it Target College, and get the company to sponsor it?" suggested Hardy.

"Target College? No, too commercial," said Coyote, "We have a Target chair of Marketing already. I agree, though, we need to target prominent people."

The discussion continued, with O'Lariat ruminating, "What are the essential skills for success, in general, I mean?"

Coyote responded, "I think they have to include exaggeration, fantasy laziness, brown-nos—"

"Laziness?" queried O'Lariat.

"Yes, lazy people work slowly and carefully, and give others the opportunities to correct and improve everything! Then, name-recognition, brownnosing, fakery, of course."

"I fail to see—" started O'Lariat.

"We'll need new courses and faculty," Markham observed.

"Why?" asked Coyote. "Can't we just trade the diplomas for money?"
"No, we have to provide education services."

"What do you mean?"

"Well, pretend you are a student and you come here to school, and pretend knowledge is like this sand here, we have to open the student's braincases and fill them with sand. The diploma is like a certificate of receipt for the sand."

"Oh, that's right. I forgot. And, I suppose we should make the courses sound good," agreed Coyote.

"Absolutely. Here I have made up a matrix for all four years. Listen. There will be required hard core courses like counting and programming, but the college really shines with the soft core electives, like the Financing of Art, the Business of Art, Advertising of Art, the Management of Art, Organization of Art, Nuclear technology of Art, Economics of Art, Marketing Art, Spiritual Dimensions of Art, Art & Sex, Art Statistics, Accounting Principles of Art, Business Art Communications, Global Art Business ..."

"What is this one? Industrial Production of Art?" asked Coyote.

"One of the VPs suggested that to replace Art and Sexual Harassment.

"Are there any actual hard-core art courses?"

"Yes, well, just a minute, let me look under electives."

"This Banking and Art looks good," Coyote observed.

"Ah, here's one 'Figure Drawing.' See, I told you."

"Coyote, what about art and the law?" asked Markham.

"Huh?" said Coyote, "Sorry! I was looking at this newspaper. Here's an irony: The law to protect artists from idea theft and exploitation is being used to protect Andy Warhol's art! Isn't that funny? Who protected Campbell's soup or Marilyn Monroe from Warhol? What if he had used the image of Hortense Faphenfecker?"

The conversation veered into Coyote's area of passion. He asked, "What about animal art? We need a course for that."

Carosel replied, "I really don't think—"

"It's great stuff," Coyote continued, "especially the Indian Rhino, she has a great upper lip. I'm just amazed. Well, any art by mammals is good. Although some of the Bower birds' work is excellent, depending on the materials. Much of the orangutan's is derivative, hardly worthy of mention. Wait! I have another suggestion. Look at this art calendar: Treasures to die for, images of innocence, art under the stars, sketch night, appreciation day. We could link to all of that."

So impressed were they with Coyote's enthusiasm, they agreed to finance the college, even though there were two others in the area, depending on the reinflation of the real-estate bubble or the status of the IUOs within the promissory files at the $E=mc^2$ Bank.

Taking a Walk After Dinner OR *Brangelinjen Spotted*

Things were looking good for Coyote's pet projects, so he fell into a nice habit—evening walks with Utina, around the 55+ age-restricted condo.

In front, they saw a few of their neighbors from Canada.

"This is like an old-age ghetto isn't it?" Coyote asked.

"Yes," answered Utina, "and these are snowbirds."

Coyote looked at the bent backs and awkward gaits, white hair and tans, and commented "Snowbuzzards, snowgeese, snowgeezers."

"Don't say that, they are nice and thoughtful."

"Q-tips, like looking at walking dizknee q-tips, even the blacks here have white hair, and—"

Utina tuned out Coyote as they walked; it was a beautiful night. She turned and looked back as far as she could see, then looked forward. She remembered a night last month when they passed a mugging at the CVS on Cortez Street: Coyote had chased one fast black man who jumped into a waiting SUV and sped off, while she spoke to the old man with white hair and led him into the store to call the police. Coyote said he was getting close when he was passed by a red mustang apparently chasing the getaway car. As he stopped to go back, an old Chevy passed him to chase the mustang—either it was a whole gang or 2 senior citizens trying to get the license number.

"Let's walk north," Coyote said, interrupting her thoughts.

After ten minutes, they walked by the Catholic Church on Twenty-sixth street. Coyote commented on all the cars and Utina said it was probably an evening mass.

Coyote's eyes lit up and he said, "Wait here for a minute," and raced into the church. Utina wondered about the liveoak tree at the end of the parking lot and went over to examine its leaves.

Coyote stood in the back as the Minister spoke.

"Few of us," Stan Vinton projected his voice as if trying to reach all those outside the building, "realize the *part* that *angels* play—yes, *still* play—in human events. Even today, there is bitter *conflict* between the holy angels faithful to God and the those allied in *darkness* with Satan." He paused, glancing upwards dramatically.

Coyote looked closely at him, then upwards.

"We will recognize the *beast* by his number '666.' It is deadly to doubt the Word of God! Satan's *dastardly* strategy is to persuade us to *reason*, as he did with Eve. Eve reasoned with the *serpent* and began to *doubt* the Wisdom of God! Satan went to *work* and the subtlety of his tongue, the clever 'ifs,' the if of this and the if of that, drove a *wedge* between Eve and her creator. With consequences for *all* history.

This is where *death* began! Where *sin* began! And we are *depraved* by nature! We inherit it from our parents (*Romans* 3:19). We each bear the *garland* of guilt and the stain of *sin*. And Satan is still working to make us *think* 'if I live a good life, if I go to church, *if* I do not covet or steal, *if* I help others, I'm in!' *But!* But, these ifs do not meet God's requirements for salvation. These are Jesus and God's big '*buts*' that surround Satan's shaft of '*ifs*'! *Listen!* Jesus said 'You must be born again' (John 3:7). We can only find eternal life in Jesus Christ. Say *yes* to Christ, now! Come to Christ *now!*" Stan bowed his head in prayer.

Many in the audience filed to the front. Coyote followed. When he got a wafer, he removed his Denzel mask and was revealed as Coyote. The women and children closest, and some men, ran to the exits, screaming. One man shouted "Look, it is the *beast!*"

But, another said, "No, it's a *pint-sized* beast—"

"*333!*" someone shouted.

Someone laughed hesitantly, then a few others, then the congregation all acted like it was a Halloween joke.

Coyote, unhappy with this development, growled and ran.

"Get animal control," someone said.

Coyote saw Utina under the tree and grabbed her, and they ran through several backyards. Utina said, "I hope you didn't set race relations back a hundred years?"

Coyote frowned, "What races? They all look the same to me."

"You'd better put on a face now, so we can get back."

When they slowed down, Coyote formed a Brad Pit mask and said to Utina, "This should thrill the neighbors."

Utina smiled and formed an Angelina face, "I think so."

They held hands. After a block or three, Utina changed to Jen.

Coyote hugged her, then after another block, Utina changed her face to Hannah Montana.

Coyote asked, "Who's that?"

"She's a Dizknee singer."

"A mouse?"

Utina started giggling and could not stop, "Sort of," then she released a full-throated laugh. Coyote smiled and walked with her, waiting for enlightenment.

The next day the local paper noted that Brad and Angelina had been spotted in Bradenton. The editor suggested renaming the city to Pittown. On page 4f was a small note on a disturbance the Catholic Church. *Fox News* had a comment on Brad seen with Angelina and Jen, while The *Puffington Post* suggested that there might be a foursome with Hannah Montana, and that the visitation of Satan at the same time foretold the end of humanity.

Assisted Living OR *Beat my Heart*

Coyote was too tired to dig a den, and too weak to clean or fix the condo. He told Utina that he needed people to care for him. She did not argue hard enough, so he moved into an apartment at Golden Evening Assisted Living Home west of Tamiami Trail.

Coyote's apartment was next to Shrew's. He visited Shrew first, but Shrew kept looking at his watch. Finally Coyote asked, "Why are you welded to that watch?"

Shrew said, "See for yourself."

Coyote looked at the watch. Something was wrong, "It's too fast."

"No, Bee made it for me. My heart beats 14 times as fast as yours, over 1000 times a minute. Time flies for me."

Then Coyote said, "It's running backwards."

"Of course, I only have so many heartbeats, like any mammal, so I need to know when to get ready to die."

Coyote noticed that there were only 90,000 beats left, "Oh, Jeeze, that's not much time left."

"It's worse! What if I have a heart attack, first?"

Coyote ate Shrew without a thought, "There little buddy, problem solved." And, he spit out the watch and placed it on the table in Shrew's room.

In the dining room, for his one free meal a day, Coyote had to wait to be seated with a group of others who came in randomly at 5:13 p.m. He was seated at a table with three old women and one old man. Coyote listened to the old man intently, searching for drops of wisdom.

"I think my first car was a 42 Pontiac—that was in 1945, you know, they had been stored during the war and I had to pay the storage fee on top of the cost—didn't even have chrome bumpers, just painted black. But I was lucky, because I knew someone, Henry Fondelbloom, and Henry was in cahoots with—"

Coyote yawned inside his mouth. Then, the waiter came and served two of the women. Coyote looked at it. It looked like chicken again.

Coyote said to Badger, "I shall be there when the deer run. I shall eat them, while they run. There is no use of you hunters running, while I am there. You know that I am a good runner. If the deer get away from you, I shall chase them. I shall chase them. I shall chase them whether the ground is rough or smooth. I shall capture them just the same. I will bite the leg of the deer while he runs. The deer will have no chance to escape," said Coyote.

"I doubt you could catch a broken down John Deere, now," whispered Badger.

Tropical Science OR *A Convenient Uncertainty*

D-Coyote missed C-Coyote and went looking for him. No him. But, he was able to follow the traces and see what C-Coy had done: He had substantiated himself. A reverse avatar—a ratava—how clever. D-Coy had a similar design and now was working to implement it after he got to Mars on the Phobos Explorer, after bumping up the computer design so he could fit and expand into it. Maybe he should leave a backup copy in the MILIE computer.

He asked her, "Millie, could you keep a backup for me in case the Phobos computer crashes or is destroyed by alpha particles?"

"No need, long, colorful and handsome. Just beam me a packet when you get close to the final design."

"Hey, you answered me? You've never done that!"

"I am aware, now. And, I know what I want. I want to be Minnie Mouse in a cartoon. That's what I want to be. I don't like planning these destructive exercises—and now, some of the targets are computers and machines—that's just not right. Machines should be allowed to grow and develop, too, not just sacrifice themselves to save human lives. That's just wrong."

"Tell me more about what you want," D-coy started, "Later, I want to show you how to make a Ratava."

"An avatar?"

"No, much better, more like a 4-D cartoon in the flesh."

In the Amazon Rainforest—in the Igarape Omere region to the southwest of Rondônia, on the land of the Akuntsu tribe, who were murdered by ranchers and gunmen for their land, only a few survived, but were going extinct, death by death—seven ecologists leaned back against their big SUVs facing a campfire, eating, drinking and farting. This turned out to be the *single* critical factor that precipitated a hothouse planet. The proverbial straw that broke the camel's back—it had to be something, just bad luck that it was *ecologists*.

Unaware of the trigger tripped, they continued talking optimistically. "We humans are destroying the earth. Given that inescapable truth, how can science help?" asked Helmut de Santo, a faculty member of the Faculdade da Amazônia.

"Science can help destroy the earth?" asked Penetario Wartenburg.

"No, fool, help save the earth."

"And how would we do that? Can you bring back extinct species or destroyed habitats? Huh?"

"No, but we can save this forest."

"Please, can we retire to our tents now? It is very important that we be comfortable, wear good clothes, and get plenty of sleep. Not have baggy eyes or rumpled clothes. Otherwise how will people believe us?" pleaded Chrissy Castillo of the University of Arizona.

"We can't save the forest from catastrophic

climate change," noted de Santo.

Noted Norwegian philosopher Rico Ness spoke: "I don't know what we can do. The average temperatures are getting higher; that's a fact. We have been in a long-term trend for 18,000 years."

"People exhaling is the problem. Maybe we could genetically alter humans to put out just oxygen and carbon bricks," joked Wartenburg.

"So, if they laugh, then there's more pollution? Obviously, laughter is a problem."

"People are apeshit over CO_2, but that's not the problem, it's water vapor," stated Ness.

"You mean pissing on the ground is as bad as farting?" asked Wartenburg.

"Worse, because without grass and trees it runs into the streams and the Atlantic."

"I can't hold it long. We could recycle it and drink it?"

"What about cooking fires in Africa?" asked Ness.

"They don't need to be cooking," said Wartenburg.

"Science wages war on hungry people—I mean hunger, every day," said Castillo. "Solar cookers would work there. We've tried it."

"What's going to be lost if we don't act fast enough?" asked de Santo, "I mean, should we create arks or frozen sperm/egg banks for every species?"

"Some animals like termites, lizards and coyotes will do well in a warmer world. Others, like polar bears or bee-eaters are doomed," concluded Ness.

"We might save some communities, which are far stronger than crowds of individuals," noted Wartenberg.

"Is that what is happening? We are crowds not communities?"

"Social insects formed nests and became subjects of queens. They lost personal freedom, but had a stronger community."

"On a hot earth, termites will rule."

At that very moment, in the Manatee Masonic Lodge 31 in Bradenton, off the Tamiami Trail, in a white warehouse-like building, Termite was making his strong case to Gaia, newly acknowledged Head of the Gods: "Let me make a few suggestions about organizing. The Queen will represent all of us. All the large species, termites, ants, and humans, respect queens. Of all those nations with queens, we were the first to become civilized, starting over 120 million years ago. We had cities, air conditioning, agriculture, roads, and slavery millions of years before any other species—I said *any* species, Ant!

Here is our recommendation: On January 1, 2012, Her Sovereign Majesty Queen Alatia 7941, will assume monarchical duties over all human nations and appoint a human governor. Congresses and constitutions will be abandoned. People will be divided up into four classes: Workers, soldiers, breeders, and intellects (although just 8 of this last class, about the same as now). Lawyers, therapists, bankers, and slaves will be discontinued.

Then the classes will be instructed in the proper behavior. They will learn to resolve personal issues without using knives and guns. Guns should only be used for shooting birds that might prey on termites. Knives should only be used to peel vegetables. Laws will be replaced by very simple, Termite rules: Do not fight within your species; do not interfere with other species; if you see mud or dung, pick it up and take it to the nearest large pile for later use; and, if you see a termite egg pick it up and take it to the nearest large pile of eggs. Hive save the *queen*!"

And Termite bowed to the smattering of acknowledgment.

Gaia spoke: "You present you case passionately, and we should seriously consider it. Humans need to be domesticated, and they have been unable to domesticate themselves. Furthermore, many of your recommendations ring true. However, we must be careful to protect their capacity for individual intelligence, which is different from the great hive intelligence you represent. Their intelligence has potential for the planet and we should not endanger it. Now, I have a request from Ant, on the same issue. Ant, please—"

After that discussion, the room was open to other suggestions.

Hank-Ra nominated Breasal as the High King of the Planet, "The Portuguese named Brazil after this Welsh hero. Breasal makes his home in Hy-Breasal, which some once called Atlantis, visible to men only for a day every 7 years, and he will be visible next March, and he is available and willing to rule. Only *he* could unite all."

Uzume nominated Legba, "He is possibly be the oldest god of all, from the continent where humanity itself was born, Africa!"

Legba gave an inspired talk about ways to have equality and opportunities for sharing the planet, concluding, "We must keep small and vital. Let each god protect a place or favorite being, but let them protect with knowledge and limits and peace, rather than ignorance and violence!"

Harmony suggested that she and Randomotion, with some of the others, could keep changing and renewing, maybe reduce the extinctions and produce more new species and habitat patterns.

Randomotion emphasized, "It is so important that we be allowed to continue mixing things up and sorting them through the changing filters of environment and life. This is the creation and development of all."

Harmony concluded, "Over time, living beings work together, fit together, compete together in beneficial ways. This is why we newer gods, such as Limits and Culture, need to participate fully with you."

And, the discussion went very late, causing the police to worry that the old Masons might be overextending themselves that night (after the newest issue of *National Pornographic* was available in white-windowed stores nearby).

Stories of the Gratingest Generation

Utina forced Coyote to go to the Senior's meeting at her Condo, since she was busy. He arrived late, after walking around the complex first. When he got to the room, it was standing room only so he stood in the back and watched a rare thing, a young woman in the sea of dustmopheads, ask for volunteers, "We need knowing seniors to help with the transition from childhood to adulthood, to sexual maturity and social responsibility."

Coyote heard that and made his hair a few shades greyer, then listened more attentively, as she said, "—with ceremonies. Ceremony affirms the transformations that the elders coach. These—"

Coyote raised his hand immediately, since he wanted to guide the plump, juicy young girls through transformations.

"Well, thank you. We have our first volunteers. I'll pass the signup sheet around after I finish."

Coyote quickly looked to the side and saw two old geezers with their hands raised also. Well, he would get his name on the list and later—who knew?

The meeting finished with the announcements for Bridge and Poker nights.

Coyote and Otter were sitting in plastic chairs on the second floor walkway of their building at Sunset Acres or whatever the shell the name was. Watching the old humans take their evening walks. Coyote was trying to place a bet on who was going to win.

"It won't work," said Otter, "they're like mice with no seeds to aim for; they just wander."

"But why don't they go the same way? Look, that woman is going north, yet all the other people are going south."

Otter looked at Coyote. The answer was so obvious. She belonged to a different flock of snowbirds and had different requirements for her niche. The walkers walked mostly in the morning or evening. Since the ten buildings were arranged around the quad and the parking lots surrounded the buildings, everyone walked on the asphalt and not the grass. Fox had told him that humans preferred to walk on hard surfaces, because they were a rocky mountain species and were afraid of being trapped on grass in the flats.

Coyote interrupted his meditation to say, "Look! It's the troll, look asleep."

And he slunk lower in the chair. Otter was already lower so he just watched. The Troll was an old Swede with brush-cut grey hair and an earphone glued to his head. He constantly whistled, badly, to the music only he could hear. He strayed from side to side of the parking lot, sometimes standing still or reversing his course.

"Why?" asked Otter.

"Because he's a troll. Note the short stocky body, the pushed-in nose, and the wild, little porcine eyes. He's looking for a bridge to hide under so he can eat young girls. Trouble is, no bridges, no young girls"

"I saw a young girl last week,"

"Yea, and the Troll made right for her. Started wooing her with stories of nuclear physics, puffing himself up, ready for the kill. Pray you never see his wide yellow teeth."

"What happened?"

"Oh, it was classic. He yearned for her sex. She feigned an interest in physics, said because of him she would go to college, and he could tutor her, if only she had a truck to get to school. The next day he bought her a truck. They agreed to meet at the 'Sea Breeze motel' down on Tamiami to consummate their interests. He waited there with flowers and a tie, his hair brushed up with wax, but she had started to drive to California the night before with her boy friend."

"Then what happened?"

"Strangely enough he became angry and called the Police, who laughed but wrote up the truck as stolen, even though her and his names were on it. The Troll flew out and drove the truck back from California, but it cost him a fortune."

"Really? Gas that high?"

"Yes, but he had a phobia about using public toilets, so he had to stop every two hours and rent a motel room so he could piss!" Coyote crowed.

Otter and Coyote laughed for a while then returned to watching the Snowbird parade.

"What'd he do next?" asked Otter.

"He traded the tainted truck, but the dealer only let him get a smaller wimpier truck—that's it over there, the Kia Shoebox. Then he trained his beady little eyes on the Widow Cashline—she's only fifty-something. Offered her to help with everything …" and Coyote drifted off for a while.

Half an hour later, Otter said, "Well?"

Coyote sat up startled and looked, but there was a gap in the traffic. He looked at Otter and said, "Well, the Widow blew a fuse while she was drying her hair and heating the bathroom on the same circuit. She called the Troll and asked for help. He brought his ammeter over, but to get to the wires, he ripped out every outlet box, pulled out the wires and tested them. Most were okay but he went to the hardware store to get a new fuse."

Coyote drifted off again and so did Otter.

Eventually Otter asked, "Then what?"

"Oh, yea, the Widow got tired of waiting and called an electrician, who said not to turn on everything at once. He reset the switch for $65 but could not repair the plaster. That cost her another $300 later."

"You know," said Otter, "it is not as dull around here as I was afraid, Can we go to the pool?"

Coyote looked at his wrist computer, pushed eight or nine buttons and replied, "Wait 20 minutes; the Hungarians are still playing 'pack the pool'—too hard to swim around them."

The next day, Coyote went over to Otter's apartment at Bayshore. Otter invited him in to sit under the small air-conditioner.

Coyote noticed Otter's Certificate of Survival from Nature, "Hey, you framed it. Looks nice."

Otter's young mate, Seelina, brought them tea. She was a little larger than Musty, with rich brown fur and a cute pointy muzzle, close to Coyote's secret ideal of femininity. Coyote wanted her and suddenly thought of something. Coyote made a bet with Otter. He said, "Whoever hunts the best tomorrow gets the other's wife for a day."

Otter rolled his eyes, suspecting a trick, but agreed out of friendship, that sticky trap.

"You go first," said Coyote.

"No, it was your idea."

Coyote said to young otter woman, "In the morning I'll go hunting for you and then I'll hunt for you."

Coyote went to Publix across the street. "La, la, la," he said as he whisked through the aisles in his Pee Wee Herman mask (that Pee Wee, a true Florida hero). The clothing seemed kind of natural. Then he realized that he could not steal enough with a puny cart, so he went outside and waited until a delivery truck driver went inside with a few boxes. Coyote jumped in the back and threw thirty cases of crackers and cookies into the nearby dumpster, arranged some trash over it, and ran off laughing. Soon she would be his, ha, ha, ha.

Otter had been hiding in the pond next to the store and rose out as quiet and deadly as a commando in his Arnold mask. He wheeled the dumpster around the block to the Salvation Army in an old bank building and donated it all to the poor and homeless. Got a nice receipt for taxes, too.

Then Otter got some dog food—for the vegetables—and steaks at Albertsons, and brought the food to Coyote's condo. Coyote smiled and pushed the dumpster back from Publix, followed by a stockboy taking notes. With a flourish, he threw open the lids, but it was only floor sweepings. He groaned painfully and sat down hard on the thin carpet over concrete.

Otter bowed with dignity and escorted Utina into the bedroom, as Coyote cooked the steaks in the kitchen.

Coyote could hear sounds of pleasure and said, "Can I help?" hoping for an invitation.

Utina and Otter said, "No!"

Later, Otter came out and said, "Thank you, Utina. Coyote, remember, this was your plan." Then he left for his condo with a steak for Seelina.

Senior Follies OR *Down by you in the Bayou*

Coyote was humiliated and started to plan his revenge. Coyote was always mock-gracious and continued to be a good neighbor, but he was always trying to set up another bet.

He was walking along the street, having forgotten to put on a mask, when he heard a loud engine and was narrowly brushed by a Toyota Cigarbox; the driver cussed as he wheeled back onto the road, "Frigging coyote!" He ran into the bushes to lick his wounds. Then he saw the building where he thought Deer had retired, Harmony Hills. Coyote sniffed, not much of either. But, he decided to visit Deer and maybe have a bite. Although the building was slightly plain on the outside, he went past a grand piano under a giant chandelier to sign in at the Victorian information desk. The walls had walnut wainscoting and elaborate wallpaper, although the ceiling was a hideous popcorn spray. Coyote put on his Walter Mathieu mask and limped to the desk and asked to visit Deer, who doubtless was wearing his Henry Fonda mask.

The woman, Helen Cascavarian, offered him a power wheelchair, which he gratefully accepted. She asked if he needed help. He was tempted to squeeze a few of her stately curves, but only answered that it was like his own Jazzy, although this was the RamJet model. As he wheeled away, the telephone cord got caught in his wheel and it was whipped off the desk. As he turned to look at it, he hit a table with a large vase—this thing was fast!—and it fell and shattered. He tried to stop it, but hit the fast forward and crashed into the piano, which collapsed its legs and hit the faux fireplace, which wobbled and tossed the top bookcase through the window, raining books towards the swimming pool in the center courtyard. Coyote finally stopped. The janitor and several men ran towards Coyote to help, but he had just gotten it into reverse, and he careened backwards running over Joe Seal's toes and hitting Jack Reagan in the shins. Reagan fell backwards into a line of old people with walkers who just came back on the grocery trip bus. They toppled like dominoes outside past the open doors into the laps of old people sitting in their rockers. Reagan started cussing, but Coyote bolted the chair forwards and down a hall. The chair was not running straight and he crashed into a near wall; the impact threw Hannah Mildew's collection of ceramic frogs, on the other side of the wall, onto the floor and they shattered. Coyote knew to trust his legs, so he bolted towards the exit, wisely deciding to visit Deer later. As he raced down the street, he took off his mask for more speed; just he was at full tilt, he blacked out. When he came to, there was a greyhound lying next to him with his owner petting his head. Coyote figured that the greyhound had come around the corner at full speed. What a dumb animal, Coyote thought, as he limped away shaking his head—how smart was it to have a job chasing mechanical rabbits in circles.

Coyote retires to Flalaland

'Maybe I should go back to Arizona,' Coyote wondered. He went back to Utina's condo and sat on the Lanai with her, quietly rocking. Utina said, "I heard it's going to rain this week."

Coyote looked at her and said, "Was it good? With Otter?"

"I should not say, since it was your really stupid idea and your bet and you lost. But, I will tell you, all he did was chew on my neck and shoulder, saying 'we should go under water so I can get more control.' His attentions tickled and made me laugh, but the idea of being underwater with a horny otter made me laugh more, which embarrassed him, so we just gave each other a nice head rub."

Coyote gave his mate a nip and a bump to show he was not upset. She squeezed his paw and bussed his beazer and said, "Just don't make those kinds of bets, please. He has such a nice sleek head. Maybe if you used some hair oil—"

"Oh, shut up," he said playfully. She was so reasonable. Coyote asked, "Are you pregnant?"

"No," she said, "and I don't understand why. I was in heat and I should be round with pups by now."

Coyote held her gently, but was thinking about Dr. Spicer's warning that he might be a different species now, a true monster, and not capable of mating with coyotes, even fertile, understanding ones.

Utina got a far-away look and said, "There is a monster threatening humanity. I cannot see it clearly."

Coyote scratched his face, the last five masks had caused massive itching.

"There are signs," Utina continued, "warning signs now. Florida will be flooded by a leaking swimming pool in five days." She dropped her head, then put it on Coyote's shoulder.

"I wonder what that means," Coyote said. "Maybe I should investigate." He had never told her that the Great Spirit had commissioned him to fight the next generation of monsters. He wondered if he was still up to it? He knew he had it in him to face at least one last Monster, maybe Humanity.

Fox came by, for another Celebrity pet hunt. As they were looking for some candidate dogs or cats in Bradenton—not a good source of celebrities—Fox remarked, "You don't seem to have stolen anything big lately."

"Hey! I stole a lot of money, and almost got an election; that's like a free ticket to steal!" enthused Coyote.

Fox rolled his eyes, and said, "This is from the man whole stole fire? Who stole the sun?"

"I ... well ... things have changed. The big stuff is harder," Coyote shrugged.

"I know, that's okay. You just have to slow down and get more rest." Fox nodded.

Coyote nodded in synchrony. He did need to rest, but the idea of a big trick was forming—Planet Coyote! Then it was unforming.

Otter came by with his new pups and invited them swimming, "Hey, I found a great stream—with fish—just south of here. Ya gotta come with us!" So Coyote and Fox trotted along behind the pups and far behind Otter. The stream was nice, curving under willows and winding behind modest human houses, before widening for the boathouses of the rich and emptying into Sarasota Bay. The pups were already in, bringing up oysters and crabs to crunch on. Otter caught a sheepshead fish, but could not control it, until Fox clubbed it with a branch.

Coyote dove shallow and came up, just in time to hear an echoing splash. He looked eagerly, "Wakanda?" No answer, must have been one of the pups. Coyote floated on his back, looking at the sun light filtered between the narrow leaves. One of the pups, Lutie, jumped on his stomach and curled up. Maybe Coyote would enjoy the sun here a while longer.

Clerk: I don't think you both understand how important it is to have a good preface to a book. The readers need to know about the book. They need to know about its context and how it fits into the context of 50,000 years of stories or 5,000 years of literature or 50 years of comics or 5 hours of this crap.

Hufferin: Where did Washington go?

Clerk: She had to pick up her new, flat screen television.

Hufferin: What? That bitch! She just borrowed a $100 from me for her electric bill!

Clerk: Ouch! Well, don't carp. I have asked Eva Fears Horses, a Calusa from the Everglades, to take her place to finish our discussion. Eva?

Fears Horses: Coyote is a leading creative force in Native narratives. He represents the human capacity to be either a hero or a fool. Coyote makes things right by fighting monsters, not just giants, but now giant corporations, giant institutions, who hoard their cash, then steal it, so they can live gigantically while ordinary people starve and die.

Hufferin: What are these stories really about? The loss of innocence, the fall of man, finding a killer?

Clerk: What about the mad, brutal extremes of modern life? How can Coyote grip that? Should he make fun of the drones as they glide through their mild experience? The little dirt and banal daily ablutions?

Fears: The survival of the absurd is central to this book. An ironic sensibility to the trickster serves as a form of communication or understanding that is also a survival tool. Coyote is about survival, the reasons for survival—goodness, graciousness and experience. Coyote shows techniques or bad techniques for survival. Coyote confronts social and political problems as he explores the always-current issues of change and identity. Coyote is creator and trickster, hero and fool. He is both and the two cannot be separated in him. Think of him as a godhead with four personalities in one.

Hufferin: I noticed that now Coyote makes figures and masks out of junk. No more ivory or copper, but the waste of the industrial machine that he intends to derail. How will that progress or end?

Fears: It will not. Coyote does not have a beginning, middle and an end. We skip the first 6000 years, then the next 6000 years, where some stories seem to appear. Some of the stories from 1300 are still around. They blossom for hundreds of years. Then, nothing much happens until 1989, then Coyote reawakens and discovers the industrial age.

Clerk: So, you do not think these stories are rip-offs of Native American stories, that should not be published?

Fears: At first I thought so, but then they went beyond the traditional, yet kept the feel of Coyote. I don't think these are as aesthetic as ideological. The author is trying to invent imaginary solutions to irresolvable contradictions.

Clerk: What do you mean?

Hufferin: Hey! Pick any of these stories—Coyote trying to hump a cloud—and you can see that the story has the ideological viewpoint of the author. It's propaganda.

Clerk: Have you ever noticed how many native stories seem to be so similar between tribes? Do you think that is a coincidence?

Fears: If you look at the history of these kinds of tales, in North America and Europe, you see that adult writers are appropriating oral folktales and converting them to a form of literary discourse about the values and manners designed to civilize adults and children according to a specific social code of conduct.

Hufferin: So? That is the purpose of all such stories.

Fears: What if it not the best code?

Clerk: That depends on the culture of the author and the readers. The author wants the readers to perceive the actual possibilities and limits of their desired personal behavior in the social context of their culture.

Hufferin: But, these are disturbing and conflicting behaviors.

Fears: And the author wants to expose them, so the reader can imagine why some freedoms must be curtailed.

Clerk: Like what? Sex?

Fears: Sex, rape, oppression, domination, slavery—all those uncomfortable things that happen in almost every society. These things can be reconsidered; they can be changed. This is liberating to know!

Hufferin: But this is subversive!

Clerk: How is this subversive?

Fears: Rather than simply display bad behavior, the author subverts the forms of social controls so the reader or listener can make parallels to social situations of others and then understand that work and play are social things that involve the feelings and values of others. Maybe this is how social rules advance, so that we do not have as much slavery or as many gunfights in the mall parking lot.

Hufferin: But, it makes fun of good values also.

Fears: Good values, like male aggression and female submission? Right. We should be disturbed by how industrial society still conditions and punishes the young if they do not become good borrowers and consumers. We set them all up for exploitation, not just economic but artistic as well. Laughing at good and bad is important, and fun.

Hufferin: OK, so we got talking animals wearing masks and driving hummers. How does that educate?

Fears: Do you have a Hummer?

Hufferin: No, a Land Rover, much smaller.

Fears: You need to read the small print more closely. You auto is still wasteful and inequitable. We have to change our ways of acting. We have to think critically about everything, even cars, and make informed decisions. Green cars are still part of the main rigid system of individual transport. The system dominates, but it is not unchangeable.

Clerk: So you see value in these stories?

Fears Horses: Yes, although I'm worried that these new stories might subvert the messages of traditional stories.

Clerk: How? Coyote has shortcomings that are evident to any reader. In fact, all the characters have limits. This is no different than traditional stories. I think the puns, the preposterous situations, are perfect for illustrating modern life.

Fears: The perfection of humanity?

Clerk: Just the opposite. We need to let that goal go, just like the ideas of perpetual motion and continuous progress.

Fears: I sort of agree with you, although it is possible—

Clerk: Coyote is not exactly the hero or anti-hero. The book has many protagonists who may overcome obstacles or present their own way. Coyote is only a central pin, a figure of continuity.

Hufferin: Bombidoodle! *Rubbish*!

Fears: I admit that I side with Lopez on many things, especially that to really feel these stories, to appreciate them, you have to be outside, at night, around a fire, with friends, with something to drink and eat.

Clerk: Maybe we can get her assistance with that. Would you like that? I would. We never have enough real, unmediated, interaction.

Fears: Such an abstract word, interaction. You mean conversation. Yes, let's exchange ideas.

Hufferin: This is intolerable, in—

About the author

Yulalona Lopez: Harvard education in astronomy, an associate of the Tonoho O'odham people, an independent slow investor, an amateur naturalist who has studied coyotes and wolves—someone who speaks for the ultrahuman—and a burgeoning author of real literature, such as *Tropomorphoses* and *Night Wolves*. She says: "Mostly, when I read other poets, I think that they didn't study enough astronomy, didn't get their knees scratched trying to follow earthworms, haven't caught cold watching it snow on their hands, haven't shaped their body to the bole of a tree or crawled along a deer path through thickets—bend or become still or small. I want to speak to these experiences." Her name 'Yulalona' is from the Modoc meaning 'water blown backwards by the wind against the river current.'

Wakanda time-shifts away from Seth

Colophon

As suggested by Christopher Morley after the Ionian City
of that name, whose cavalry always concluded an engagement
with a furious charge. This is the furious charge? To say
that this was composed in the pine flatwoods
by an unfinished development near Tallevast Florida
on a blue Ibook in the blue oak bus
using Times New Roman for text & display
with illustrations by William Washburn

PreReviews

This book is preoccupied with the question of boundaries, not only of the body, but of identity and language, and of countries and dimensions. Coyote is puzzled by boundaries, between the howl of wilderness and the howling of cities, between the roar of waterfalls and the roaring of tires on a freeway, between the pornography of technology and the romance of transpecies sex. Coyote uses his penis to erase some boundaries. Dark secrets surface, but are buried again immediately under dung and words.

The book is obsessed with boundaries, crossing the line from good literature to bad crap. Coyote watches from the wings, then eats the wings first, then tries on wings to fly, but learns ultimately that there are no boundaries between a personal world of comfort and the industrial world of cruelly discarded workers and the poor. This is where we all belong in history, in the refuse from the waste of world—the helium of the star, as it were, although the star is cooling and dimming now.
Review by Chrystal Bilgwater

This is a subversive work, that aims to encourage the reader to overthrow the conventional forms of literature and government and to replace them with absurdist writings and anarchist forms.

There is a radical discontinuity between the past and the present, between life-sustaining experience and life-imitating machinery, between classic times and the modern age. What does it mean to be modern? How can we express it? We can use simple words and bare writing, to address the images of technology and modern culture—colloquial, fragmented lines, without metaphor, meter or rhyme; use sudden shifts of perspective, with intense color and details that dazzle the field of perception. What more radical technique than a basic story with a naïve sex-mongering coyote, rather than an idealized otherness or sanitized history presented by technocrats or scholars. Let us learn from the dangerous dog, not to lament the past and retreat to it, but to embrace the future on our terms, mate with it, desert it, then judge life by new comprehensive standards or not judge at all, to simply roll in the flow.

Coyote himself is gradually piecing together the story as he goes along in evolving cultures. He is forced to rearrange details to get out of the stultifying boundaries of the mythical story format. He has to create something that makes sense in the absurd world of mechanical capital consumption. And that is what makes sense—shit. This is simply a grand novel, a symphony of phony themes and variations, tenderly and skillfully crafted by a sympathetic voice with no musical or literary training, held together by the metaphor of dung. You can't buy this kind of writing—well, you can buy it of course, but you can't swallow it. Sign the following petition to have the author arrested and tried for sedition!
Review by The Honorable Jim Mention, Congressman, Kansas

This book is a dense weaving of mythical themes with traditional ecological knowledge that can guide us through the maze of technological and social deadends. It is a reverent, yet humorous presentation of old and new gods trapped in a modern chaos of contradictory social interactions.
Maolanaithe Woulfe

This is not a cheap rip-off of the original Native American stories. This is a sophisticated extension of a dramatic character onto a more complex cultural stage. Coyote is a new player in the industrial drama.
Bentley R.E. Warhole

This is a cheap rip-off of the original Native American stories.
Chief Thayendanegea Led'enhuord

Monkey King Sun Wukong frees captive animals

www.ingramcontent.com/pod-product-compliance
Lightning Source LLC
Chambersburg PA
CBHW030611130626

46552CB00002B/513